The priest cleared his throat.

Jolie took one last look at Apostolis, soaking in this last moment of blessed widowhood before he became her husband.

He looked back, that gleaming gold thing in his gaze, but his expression unusually serious.

For a second, it was as if she could read his mind.

For a long, electric moment, it was almost as if they were united in this bizarre enterprise after all, and her heart leaped inside her chest—

"Stepmother?" he said, with a soft ferocity. "If you would be so kind?"

No, she told herself harshly. *There is no unity here. There is only and ever war. You will do well to remember that.*

And then, with remarkable swiftness and no interruption, Jolie relinquished her role as Apostolis's hated stepmother, and became his much-loathed wife instead.

Notorious Mediterranean Marriages

One arrogant Greek billionaire. One ruthless Sicilian tycoon. Two scandalous weddings!

A brand-new captivating duet from *USA TODAY* bestselling author Caitlin Crews.

As close as brothers and as powerful as gods, Apostolis Adrianakis and Alceu Vaccaro have forged their way through the world together. Now the time has come for them to marry...in the most scandalous of circumstances!

Ruthless Greek Apostolis is left no choice but to do the unthinkable. To claim his inheritance, he's forced to marry Jolie Girard—his widowed stepmother. Their hatred for each other binds them in a way no ring ever could. But there's a fine line between hate and wildly intoxicating desire...

Read Apostolis and Jolie's story in
Greek's Enemy Bride
Available now!

When brooding Sicilian Alceu shared a scorching night with Dioni Adrianakis, his best friend's sister, he had no idea their sizzling encounter would have such long-lasting consequences. And now he's giving Dioni no choice—he will find her and claim his heir!

Discover Alceu and Dioni's story,
coming soon!

GREEK'S ENEMY BRIDE

CAITLIN CREWS

PRESENTS

H Harlequin®
PRESENTS™

ISBN-13: 978-1-335-93940-1

Greek's Enemy Bride

Recycling programs for this product may not exist in your area.

Harlequin Enterprises ULC
22 Adelaide St. West, 41st Floor
Toronto, Ontario M5H 4E3, Canada
www.Harlequin.com

MIX
Paper | Supporting responsible forestry
FSC® C021394

Printed in Lithuania

USA TODAY bestselling, RITA® Award–nominated and critically acclaimed author **Caitlin Crews** has written more than one hundred and thirty books and counting. She has a master's and PhD in English literature, thinks everyone should read more category romance and is always available to discuss her beloved alpha heroes—just ask. She lives in the Pacific Northwest with her comic book–artist husband, is always planning her next trip and will never, ever read all the books in her to-be-read pile. Thank goodness.

Books by Caitlin Crews

Harlequin Presents

A Billion-Dollar Heir for Christmas
Wedding Night in the King's Bed
Her Venetian Secret
Forbidden Royal Vows
Greek's Christmas Heir

Innocent Stolen Brides

The Desert King's Kidnapped Virgin
The Spaniard's Last-Minute Wife

The Teras Wedding Challenge

A Tycoon Too Wild to Wed

The Diamond Club

Pregnant Princess Bride

Visit the Author Profile page
at Harlequin.com for more titles.

For Flo and sweet Nancy

CHAPTER ONE

IT WAS A resoundingly foul day for a wedding.

Not even the splendor of the internationally acclaimed, widely beloved wonder that was the historic Andromeda Hotel, standing proud on one of the loveliest cliffs in the Cyclades, could maintain its trademark resplendence in such a relentless downpour. It was as if the heavens above were as appalled by these particular nuptials as the participants.

Standing beside the great windows overlooking the churning sea in her wedding dress, an understated affair that she had sourced from her closet in an elegant, pearlescent dove gray—because black was too obvious—Jolie Girard felt quietly and personally vindicated.

It looked the way she felt.

But pointed gale sent from the gods as a metaphor or no, this wedding was happening. There was no doubt about that. There was no escaping it, and they'd both tried. They had more than tried.

They had both exhausted every possible legal angle. They had insulted each other in every possible way, then started all over again, and then moved on to insults that had likely left scars that only time would show. The intense arguments after the will had been read had gone on for so long that it was a shock it hadn't been noted by the ever-hovering paparazzi who had been clustered outside the hotel after the funeral.

There was nothing for it, sadly.

Jolie Girard, widow of the infamous and ancient tycoon Spyros Adrianakis—who had taken his Cretan grandfather's stately mansion on a less-traveled-to Greek island that his father had made it into a hotel and turned it into a destination that, these days, attracted only the most exclusive and glamorous clientele—was marrying the devil himself.

That being her arrogant and unpleasant stepson, Apostolis Adrianakis, who was also individually famous the world over—mostly for his excesses and colorful romantic entanglements.

Colorful was a euphemism. It was more of a swamp, in Jolie's opinion.

I will take care of you, Spyros had promised her in his last days. *Never fear, Jolie* mou, *I will see to it you are taken care of for the rest of your life.*

She should have known better than to believe him. She *did* know better.

If men could be trusted, after all, the span of her whole life would be different.

It was so dark and gloomy outside that she could see her reflection in the glass, though it was fully morning by now. She adjusted the expression on her face, because the battle was already lost. There was no point giving the irritating Apostolis, her groom, the satisfaction of imagining that she was coming to this wedding diminished in some way.

She would do the diminishing if there was any about, thank you. Just as she would do the allotted time—five eternal years of matrimonial prison—and on the other end of this nightmare, she would be free.

Jolie would finally be free. Her cousin Mathilde would also be free, because that was the bargain she'd made. And she could go off and do...whatever it was she wanted.

Maybe she would know what that was by then.

She felt a prickling down the length of her spine and then, a moment later, saw a shadow pull itself into the form of a man in the doorway behind her, like some kind of fairy-tale monster.

He was not a monster, she told herself stoutly. He only wished he was.

The truth about Apostolis Adrianakis was that he was no more and no less than a man.

Jolie intended to remind him of that, should he be tempted to believe his own press and consider himself something more akin to a deity. Or anything supernatural at all.

She turned to face him because he might not be a monster, but that didn't mean she fancied having him at her back. Might as well bare her neck and belly while she was at it—

But the visual that accompanied that thought landed...wrong.

Because she was looking directly at him as she envisioned *baring* any part of herself and *looking at him* had always been deeply problematic.

Much as she might wish otherwise, another unfortunate truth about Apostolis Adrianakis was that he was darkly gorgeous, impossibly beguiling despite his many obvious personality flaws, and almost hypnotically magnetic. Even to someone like her, who was no fan of his. It was no wonder that the better part of the earth's population followed him around with stars in their eyes.

Jolie did not believe in gods, Greek or otherwise, but it was impossible not to look at Apostolis and wonder if maybe, just maybe, they were still wandering the earth. If they had taken to islands like this one and now lurked in villages rife with celebrities and holidaymakers in the summer, whispering their own legends and myths from every charming alley. If they were made of flashing dark eyes in a shockingly beautiful face crafted to wedge itself between the ribs of anyone who dared glance his way.

Perhaps, she thought sharply, she ought to have been grateful that he came by his arrogance naturally. It was better than the alternative. She could not imagine what a chore it would be to deal with a man who imagined himself as indisputably magnificent—visually, anyway—as Apostolis, yet wasn't.

This version was trying enough.

Her erstwhile groom had decided to express himself in his choice of apparel as well, she saw. He wore the expected suit, but it looked almost as if he'd slept in it—or, knowing Apostolis, had slept with someone else on top of it. Or several someone elses.

Jolie told herself she would not care in the least if he had.

"Kaliméra," Apostolis murmured in that rough-edged drawl of his that made a meal of both his accent and the simple *good morning.* "What a perfectly hideous day to marry my wicked stepmother. A luckier man has never walked this earth, I am certain."

"The joy is all mine," she replied with a polite smile that she knew he would take as a thrown gauntlet. The flash in his dark eyes assured her he did. "Nothing could bring me more happiness than forced proximity with a man who is the human equivalent of landfill. Felicitations all around."

Apostolis laughed at that as he slouched into the room, every step liquid and low, as if he did not so much walk as *glide.* The rumpled effect was not helpful. It made her think about *how* his thick, dark hair had come to look like that, as if greedy fingers had tugged at it and run their way through it. It made her wonder if he had misbuttoned his shirt deliberately or in a hurry, or if someone else had done it for him.

Obviously she would die before she asked him. Before she gave him the slightest reason to imagine she cared when she did not.

They had come to a resigned *détente* after it was clear that no victories could be won in their situation, not even Pyrrhic ones. It was an uneasy truce at best, no good faith treaties in sight, because neither one of them wanted any part of this. Left to their own devices, they would have maintained the chilly, exquisitely *precise* courtesy that had characterized their relationship since Jolie had married Spyros through the old man's funeral and the reading of his will, then never spoken to each other or interacted again.

Apostolis had not been able to forgive his father for marrying her, a girl the same age as his sister, Dioni. A girl who his father had, in fact, met at the finishing school where Dioni and Jolie had been classmates graduating together.

And he had not been able to excuse Jolie for not accepting his unsolicited advice on the topic of the forty-year age gap between her and his father. His arguments had been, boringly, that the only reasons a girl would accept an old goat like Spyros were either because she was a victim…or a gold digger.

It had been obvious what he thought *she* was.

Or maybe, she'd told her newly minted stepson the night before her wedding back then, who was ten years older than her himself, *I just like a power dynamic.*

That was the one and only personal conversation they'd had in the seven years she'd been married to Spyros.

She had not even tried to forgive him. Jolie preferred not to think of Apostolis Adrianakis and his much-lauded cheekbones at all.

And now she was marrying him.

Jolie had no idea what she could possibly have done to deserve this fate. First her aunt and uncle's behavior, which had led to all of this, but now *this*. She suspected it involved whole previous lifetimes of wickedness, at the very least, and she only wished she could remember them. That sounded like a lot more fun.

Apostolis came to a stop beside her, looking at her only briefly before he turned his attention to the gale outside. And she turned with him, instinctually, and regretted it immediately. It seemed too pat, somehow. Too coordinated, as if she was trying to mirror him.

Or maybe it was simply that she had gone out of her way to never, ever stand this close to him before.

She wished she hadn't broken that unstated boundary that had always been between them now. Or perhaps he had broken it, but either way, it did her no favors. This close to him, she was regretfully aware of him in ways she would have liked to never, ever have comprehended. Jolie knew he was tall, of course. And that he could look lean and elegant or broodingly fit, depending on his mood or the photograph in question or even what he chose to wear. And even that he, regretfully, radiated a certain kind of charisma that she liked to tell herself was repellent.

But it was easier to convince herself of that when he was across a room, aiming nothing but freezing, pointed courtesy in her direction.

Next to him, she found that her head barely cleared his shoulder and she was not a tiny woman. Today she was wearing only moderate heels, but she was instantly aware in the way taller women were that even if she been wearing her highest stilettos he would still tower over her.

She told herself that made her feel angry.

But it didn't.

What Jolie felt was fragile. And deeply, deeply feminine in a way that probably would have shocked her if she'd allowed herself to think more about it.

But she couldn't, because he also smelled good.

Jolie could have gone the whole rest of her life without the unfortunate knowledge that Apostolis Adrianakis *smelled good*. Not too much. It was nothing overbearing. Just a hint of something not cloying enough to be cologne. A whisper of scent, something that made her think of cloves stuck in oranges, the kind of Christmas decorations she pretended she couldn't remember, from a childhood that she worked hard to forget.

Because softness had never been an option. It had been a mirage like everything else, and thinking about it did her more harm than good.

Meanwhile, she was discovering that Apostolis was also warm. It was like he was a radiator, emanating heat from where he stood—

Or maybe he is simply standing there, she lectured herself. *And here you are reacting like this.*

"Appropriate weather," he drawled from beside her. "At least we have that going for us."

She stopped thinking about *scent* and *heat* and *height,* for God's sake. "The metaphors write themselves."

When their gazes tangled together, she thought he seemed equally horrified that they had stumbled upon a moment of accord here. That was so profoundly... not them.

"I had my legal team doing an eleventh-hour rustle

through all of those nasty little clauses," Apostolis said, almost idly, looking back out toward the rain and the sea that looked so gray and uninviting today. "But it all seems iron tight, as ever."

Jolie did not bother to ask him why it was that a man of such epic and widely annotated uselessness required a legal team, allowing herself only a careless shrug. "I admire your commitment to imagining, even now, that there's some way out of this."

"I don't know what my father's relationship was with you, Jolie," Apostolis said with a certain silken, lethal note in his voice. He looked at her and it was somehow more silken. More lethal. *Disastrous,* something in her cried out, but there were too many disasters to count. And he was not finished. "I cannot account for the fact that he thought to leave me his leftovers. It will never make sense to me."

He had called her far worse things than *leftovers* in the weeks since Spyros had died. That was practically a compliment in comparison. Apostolis let his mouth curve, as if remembering with great fondness all of the names he'd come up with, and she could see that his eyes looked darker than before despite that gleam like gold in them. She knew that it was malice.

She could feel it all over her.

And she did not like the sensation. "I'm not sure why your father would think that you, who have showed no interest in anything aside from your own hedonistic pleasure in at least the past ten years, would somehow wake up the morning after his will was read with the burning desire to become a hotelier." She let her smile widen. And sharpen. "Might as well take a match and set the entirety of the hotel on fire, if you ask me."

"Yet he did not ask you." Apostolis's voice was lower than usual. Jolie was tempted to imagine that she was getting to him, but she doubted it. "Just as he did not ask me how I might feel about taking on the burden of his trophy wife. Alas, here we are anyway."

With exaggerated courtesy, he turned and extended her his elbow. "The wedding party, such as it is, is waiting. The priest is in place. You are welcome to stay in here, wishing it all away, but that will not change a thing. It will only delay it and not, as I think you know, for long."

"Oh, I'm ready," Jolie assured him, with the sort of merry laugh she used at cocktail parties. "Between the two of us, I think I'm far more prepared to deal with this sentence. I mean marriage. What is five years, after all? *I'll* still be young when we divorce."

She could admit to herself that there was a certain level of exhilaration here. They'd spent so much time these last weeks shooting at each other, looking for the right weapons to use. And it felt like a victory when she happened upon one, like now.

His eyes narrowed, and she wished she knew what it was that had actually gotten to him. Was it the fact that she would be a mere thirty-two when this farce was done? Or was it their own age differential that got to him? She had only just turned twenty-seven. She wondered if that counted as the sort of outrageous age gap he'd been so concerned with when his father had married her.

Then again, she supposed they had years to find and name each and every one of these weapons, then learn how to aim them more effectively—and directly at each other.

Mutually assured destruction. All wrapped in a lovely marital bow.

She linked her arm with his because they were both out of options, and pretended she didn't feel a single thing when she did. None of that prickling awareness. None of that unacceptable heat that made her not only too focused on him, but on herself.

On the way each breath she took made her breasts brush against the bodice of her dress. Making her feel as if she was wearing something daring when she was not.

She had learned long ago that there was no need to gild the lily, as it were. People made assumptions about her by simple dint of her presence at her husband's side. The more understated she dressed and behaved, the more fevered their imagination about what must go on behind closed doors.

And she had profited from those fevers, hadn't she? Or her aunt and uncle had. And did. And would continue to for the foreseeable future—

But she cut herself off there.

Was she disappointed that Spyros had not simply rewarded her for her part in their marriage outright? She was. More disappointed than she would ever let on, because there was no safe space for her to confide in. Though she doubted that Apostolis had any idea that she and Dioni, his sister, were close—Apostolis being the sort who made declarations and assumed that everyone leaped to obey him, without ever checking up to see if that was the case—Jolie knew better than to test that relationship.

She suspected that the other girl was able to maintain their friendship because they had tacitly agreed, long ago, not to discuss Jolie's relationship with Spyros. At all.

It had been her little secret while he was alive. It would remain her secret.

And, apparently, he had decided she would have five more years to keep up the act.

Apostolis led her from the great room, taking her through the grand old house that would be theirs, now, to maintain and run together. An enterprise that she thought almost certainly doomed to failure. So, today, she tried not to think about it.

She took in the graceful accents of the lovely old place that she had loved at first sight. Legend had it that Spyros's grandfather had built the place for the love of a young island girl he'd met and married here. Right here in this house that rose up on its cliff, an elegant presence on this end of the island. The only thing, or so the story went, that rivaled the beauty of the girl he took to wife—and made it possible for him to live apart from his beloved Crete.

It was Spyros's father who had turned the Andromeda from a family home into a hotel. Despite claims that he did so out of a desire to share the house's bounty with the public, it was well known—if rarely openly discussed—that it had far more to do with his debts than any interest in sharing the family house with outsiders.

Spyros was the one with real vision. He was the one who had spent the first part of his life turning the Andromeda into what it was today. A boutique luxury hotel that catered to exclusivity above all else. It was not advertised anywhere, save word of mouth.

What matters are not so much the words, but the mouths that form them, Spyros had liked to say.

And in his case, the mouths that spoke praise of this place were some of the most glamorous around, with lives wildly coveted and usually extensively covered in aspirational media. Too bad he had enjoyed appearances rather more than any admin work. The hotel had been in some difficulties when he'd married Jolie.

But it had been booked solid two years running now, and almost at full capacity the year before that. With repeat customers and a waiting list that grew by the day.

Spyros claimed that the hotel ran on the *myth* of itself. He therefore insisted that Jolie *act* as if all she did was waft about, catching the perfect light and making other men jealous of what they could never touch. Her *grubby little figures,* as he called her bookkeeping and actual administration of managerial duties, were always to be kept a secret.

Far better the guests should think the hotel ran itself.

Jolie agreed. Myths and legends were far more appealing than ledgers and vendors and besides, managing the hotel was the one thing Spyros let her do without supervision or much commentary.

It had been her escape. She should have known that Spyros would exact a price for that, too.

Today, their wedding was being squeezed into a morning when their current high-profile celebrity guest and his entourage had gotten stuck on another island, thanks to the storm. They had been waiting for a window just like this.

And by *waiting* Jolie meant *hoping fervently for a windowless season.*

Because here at the Hotel Andromeda, the goal was the near invisibility of not just Jolie's true role, but of all the staff. Their guests preferred to operate under the impression that it was magic at work. Intuitive, effortless magic.

A wedding between non-guests would ruin that illusion.

Jolie fixed her face into something smooth and impenetrable as Apostolis walked with her into the little room they used to serve breakfast over the sea, sometimes the odd high tea, and so on.

Waiting there, looking equal parts concerned and anxious, were their witnesses. The sum total of their wedding party and guests. Dioni, who looked as scattered as ever, her dark hair falling down from the twist she'd attempted to secure it in, and, as ever, her dress not quite in place. It had used to drive their headmistress batty. She could oversee Dioni's wardrobe and dressing herself, and yet within two breaths, Dioni would somehow have the perfect ensemble looking… unkempt. Hems frayed at the merest contact with her. Straps never stayed put. She always looked *ever so slightly* bedraggled, as if elegance was a gene and it had passed her by entirely.

It was the first moment all morning that Jolie felt emotional, and she had to fight to keep that to herself. There was no place for emotion here, not even for her only friend.

But the cure for stray feelings was to look to the other side of the room, where the man who was somehow Apostolis's dearest friend in all the world stood. There were a number of things Jolie found impossible about Alceu Vaccaro. The most glaring was the fact that he had any friends at all, but especially Apostolis. Alceu was a stern, brooding, unforgiving sort of man from Sicily, with a grim mouth and an iron gaze that she was fairly certain would make every tropical flower in Greece wilt at once if he wished it.

It was hard for her to imagine a man like that giving an international playboy and professional wastrel like Apostolis the time of day.

Much less showing up for him at this tragic mockery of a wedding.

But here they all were.

Jolie felt a bit as if she was retreating to some higher plane, where she could look down on these proceedings from afar, as Apostolis shook hands with his supposed *friend*. And had to allow that it seemed more than possible that they really were friends then, because the grim Sicilian actually smiled. Slightly.

Then Apostolis was taking her arm again and they were standing in front of the priest, who looked unduly jolly, given the circumstances.

Beside her, Dioni held a bouquet of flowers, because of course she did. She offered them to Jolie.

"Keep them," Jolie murmured. "The ceremony feels flowerless to me."

Dioni sighed. "I can't imagine a flowerless wedding," she said softly. "What's the point?"

That was another thing Jolie had always adored about her friend. She was the product of all of this wealth and outrageous consequence, rubbing elbows with some of the most extravagant people to grace the planet, and yet somehow the core of her was still so innocent. Her father had called her *matia mou,* his eyes. And he'd meant it, as far as that went for a man like Spyros.

Jolie had understood that Dioni would not have the sort of life she'd had. Dioni would be allowed to choose the life she would live. Dioni could even marry for love, if she wished.

Dioni did not have the family Jolie did, Jolie reminded herself. She was mercifully free of the kinds of pressures that Jolie had been navigating for years now. If she had to, she thought then with a certain ferocity, she would do whatever she could to keep it that way.

The same way she kept her cousin safe, she would do it for Dioni, too. If she needed to.

Though she supposed that would not be necessary. Apostolis could be a monster, it was true, but not where his little sister was concerned.

The priest cleared his throat.

Jolie took one last look at Apostolis, soaking in this

last moment of blessed widowhood before he became her husband.

He looked back, that gleaming gold thing in his gaze, but his expression unusually serious.

For a moment, it was as if she could read his mind.

For a long, electric moment, it was almost as if they were united in this bizarre enterprise after all, and her heart leaped inside her chest—

"Stepmother?" he said, with a soft ferocity. "If you would be so kind?"

No, she told herself harshly. *There is no unity here. There is only and ever war. You will do well to remember that.*

And then, with remarkable swiftness and no interruption, Jolie relinquished her role as Apostolis's hated stepmother, and became his much-loathed wife instead.

CHAPTER TWO

THE NIGHT BEFORE his travesty of a wedding took place, Apostolis Adrianakis dreamed that he dug up his own father's grave, when he knew full well—while awake—that his father had been cremated and his urn placed in the family crypt. Still, he found himself out on an unfamiliar cliff beneath a strange moon, digging in the dirt with his hands. Once he reached the coffin, the old man had been hale and hardy.

And laughing.

Why are you doing this to me? Apostolis had demanded, with the temper he had deliberately never showed his father when he'd been alive. *This is how a father treats his only son?*

You are welcome, my boy, Spyros had replied.

And kept on laughing.

Now it was done, and if the old man was still laughing from the Great Beyond, the good news was that Apostolis could not hear him.

The terms of his father's will had been a stunning blow, to put it mildly, and he could not say that he had covered himself in anything approaching glory.

In order to lay claim to the Hotel Andromeda and

the estate, the lawyer had droned out, as if he was parceling out the tchotchkes instead of ruining lives, *my only son, Apostolis, and my widow, Jolie, must act as follows: marry within three weeks of this reading, run the hotel together as a seemingly happily married couple for five complete calendar years, which will entail cohabitation with no gaps of more than two weeks at a time, with no more than one such gap every quarter.*

He had been certain both he and that woman, his father's hateful wife, would *implode* with the same fury when the lawyer stopped and looked at them, as if expecting the same. But they had not. It had not been pleasant, and he could not look back upon those first few moments without mortification, but it had also not escalated to anything but a few words he supposed they'd both kept to themselves for good reason during her marriage to his father.

He despised himself for counting that as a victory.

But then again, he had never met a woman, or any other person alive, who gnawed through his carefully erected barriers and boundaries to stick her claws in deep the way his stepmother did. And always had. Without even seeming to try.

Yet despite all that, they had cleared the first objectionable hurdle. Now what remained was the grim march through the next five years, chained together in infamy. The heir to one of the great Greek fortunes... and one of the most notorious women in Europe, a subject of furious speculation and gossip since she'd married his father, a man at least forty years her senior.

And more, they were to *seem happy.*

Oh, joyous day, Apostolis thought darkly.

Neither he nor Jolie had indicated the slightest interest in any kind of reception, given how little there was to celebrate in this disaster. But his sister, forever too sunny and hopeful for her own good, ignored their rather loudly stated wishes in that respect. The moment the wedding was done, she clapped her hands together and announced that she had a surprise for them all. And sure enough, out came a wedding breakfast that Dioni clearly expected them all to partake in as if this was a regular wedding between lovebirds.

He had thought his friend Alceu, more of a brother, really, might explode.

But no one said *no* to Dioni. Not even the usually unmovable and eternally brusque Alceu, and so here they sat. *Breakfasting.* Together.

Dioni chattered on about nothing and everything, though it was difficult to tell if she was nervous or just Dioni. Alceu stared stonily back at her in aggrieved silence. And Apostolis and his brand-new *wife* fairly hummed with indignation and malice.

Or perhaps that was just him.

"You must make a toast," Dioni told his friend when the meal that no one had really touched seem to be drawing to its inevitable and painful finish. In that the food was finally going cold. "I have it on great authority that sometimes the best man, or the *koumbaros* since we are Greek—"

"I will pass on that honor," said Alceu at once. Icily.

"But as it turns out, I would love to make a speech,"

Apostolis found himself saying. Beside him, he didn't so much *see* Jolie stiffen. But he felt it. And truly, nothing could have pleased him more. "I can't tell you how it felt to discover that my birthright is not only no longer mine, but is to be shared with a woman whose notoriety exceeds my own to such an extreme degree."

He didn't stand. Instead he lounged back in his chair, lifting his glass in the direction of his blushing forced bride, who was not actually blushing. She looked the way she always did, to his endless frustration. Angelic and untouched, when she was obviously neither. As if she floated high above all the messes she'd helped make and could not possibly be called to account for any of them.

Maddening woman.

"Seven years ago, we sat around a similar table, grasping for felicitations and platitudes, while congratulating my darling wife on her first marriage. Is it a May/December romance when it encompasses four decades? Or is that more of a January/December?" He smiled as if he was enjoying himself. And discovered that, in fact, he was. "I should be flattered that my erstwhile stepmother even considered lowering her standards, and her minimum age gap requirements, to a mere *single* decade."

"I didn't lower my standards at all," Jolie said with a limpid sort of serenity that seemed to scratch all over his body, like fingernails. "It has nothing at all to do with my standards. It has to do with honoring my late husband's will."

"I think it has to do with greed," Apostolis corrected her with a lazy smile that he doubted reached his eyes. "I suppose that it is possible that you fell head over heels in love with a man who just happens to be so many years your senior and also, coincidentally I am sure, unimaginably wealthy to boot. I am told that lightning strikes where it will, though I confess I have been thus far unenlightened. But I will confess, Jolie, that I have always imagined that your motives are far more...prosaic."

His sister was staring at him with wide and distressed eyes. "So far, Apostolis, this is not a very good toast."

But he was only warming to the topic, and there was a kick to it, like particularly good spirits. "I must salute you, my lovely stepmother and wife, for managing to fall in love so *practically.*"

If he expected this to shame her, and he could admit that he did, he was destined for disappointment. Jolie reached for her own glass and sipped from it as if she needed a bit of the bubbly stuff to ward off the press of ennui. "Perhaps your sister never told you that our headmistress used to tell us, with great sincerity—and especially when we were all pining away for the grubby sort of boyfriends we imagined we wanted at the time—that an elegant woman always keeps in mind that it is just as easy to fall in love with a rich man as a poor one, and only one of those choices leads to a life of grace and comfort."

"It's true," Dioni agreed, with a nod. "She did say that. Quite a lot, actually. Though I always wondered why she hadn't gone off and married herself a wealthy man, then, if it was all the same and by her telling, such men were just littering the earth like overripe fruit."

Beside her, Alceu aimed an incredulous and frigid look at Dioni. *"Overripe fruit?"* he repeated in tones of censorious amazement.

But Dioni was not even remotely cowed. She didn't look as if she recognized that she should be.

"Like rotting stone fruit," she said merrily, in a conversational aside to Alceu as if she truly believed he wanted to continue that tangent. "Strewn about the dirt of Europe, by her telling."

Apostolis carried on before his oldest and best friend stroked out. He aimed his glass and his smile at Jolie once again. "When I first heard the terms of the will I wanted to burn the entire hotel to the ground." That got the murmurs of shock he wanted, though only from his sister. But at least she was no longer ranting on about fermenting fruit. He continued. "To save it, somehow, from the unsavory claws of a woman whose ambition must clearly outreach my own in every possible way, since she managed to end up with half of my inheritance."

Jolie, the picture of angelic serenity, let out a tinkling laugh that sounded more like bells than any human should. "In fairness, my dear stepson and husband, if you're speaking of your ambition that is a very low bar."

Apostolis laughed. Dioni stared at her plate as if it had just occurred to her that forcing them all together like this was not the best idea she'd ever had. Alceu, meanwhile, looked as if he was seriously contemplating hurling himself out the window and off the side of the cliff, for which Apostolis would certainly not blame him.

But none of that made him want to stop. He was enjoying this too much. He was finally saying all the things he'd wanted to say for weeks. For years. Forever. He'd always held back, beyond the odd, inevitable comment here and there. Even at the reading of the will he'd kept himself from a deep dive into *all* of the things he'd kept to himself over the years, because he'd still had hope that he could contest the damned thing. He was not about to squander this opportunity. They could *seem happy* tomorrow. "I have to ask myself what exactly I did that he should force the two of us to marry. That he should make the ownership of this hotel, and therefore the bulk of his estate, contingent on you and I making it through five miserable years together. Acting the part, of course, as the myth demands. I cannot imagine it, but I assume that I will soon be the recipient of the sort of tricks that lead a man to make such rash decisions. I'm expecting nothing short of Cirque du Soleil."

His sister, bless her, looked confused. His friend politely averted his gaze.

His wife smiled in that way she had that looked polite enough if a person didn't know her, but felt like razors. And if a person did know her even a little bit, well then. It was easy to see the shine of the blade.

"What is the saying?" she asked in a musing sort of tone. "Ah, yes, it goes something like, *not my circus, not my monkeys,* I think."

"But do you not see?" Apostolis made a grand gesture with his wineglass, encompassing the two of them. "This *is* the circus, Jolie. And you and I are nothing but monkeys who must dance, for five long years, as my father has a revenge I did not know he wished to take upon me from beyond the grave."

"I think he thought he was being kind," Dioni offered.

But neither Apostolis nor Jolie looked over at her.

Because Jolie, Apostolis was perhaps too delighted to see, was not holding on to her calm, angelic demeanor quite so tightly as before. "What astonishes me is that you imagine this is something *I* lobbied for," Jolie said with a different sort of laugh. Less bells, more mayhem. "After seven years of marriage, I expected a settlement commensurate with the time and effort I put in. I did not expect there to be further hoops to jump through. I certainly did not expect that I would be forced to indulge in a charity case, with a man of low character, far lower morals, and a reputation so dire that it would make the average howling alley cat seem like a cloistered monk."

"Are we discussing morals?" Apostolis asked, with true delight moving through him, like that lightning striking him after all. "Do you dare?"

"As I believe I made clear to you seven years ago and every year since in one way or another, it's not your business. It wasn't then, it wasn't at any point along the way, it isn't now." Jolie, he discovered in that moment, got colder when she was angry. Her temper was like a blast of ice but, perversely, he felt warm. And warmer by the second. "And it will never be your business, because it has nothing to do with you."

"Except behold." Another grand, sweeping gesture between them, because he could see it annoyed her. "His will made it my business and now you are also my business as well as my stepmother *and* wife, for my sins."

Jolie made a disdainful noise. "I categorically reject the idea that your sins, voluminous and colorful as they undoubtedly are, should be rewarded. Not even your father, who had an alarming soft spot for your antics, would consider those antics worthy of anything but a sigh and a trip through his own memories of sordid seasons past." She eyed him as if he had woken up this morning something less than his usually resplendent and tempting self when he knew very well he had not. "Upon reflection, all I can think is that your father was so certain that you were not up to the job of handling his estate and the Andromeda that he realized you needed training wheels, if you will. A guiding hand. And since he knew that no one in their right mind would take on such a job, he made certain that I had no other choice but to guide you as best I can."

Apostolis laughed at that, and kept laughing, though it was more a flash of that fury that had been a fire inside him since the will was read than anything approaching amusement. That she dared to harp on and on as if *he* was a failure of a man. As if *his* sins were so terrible when she could not possibly know the truth about him *or* Spyros and *her* hands were not exactly clean either.

Though the fact his own father had chosen to believe the stories about him was, he was forced to acknowledge, something he had never done enough to combat.

The truth was never as salacious as it appeared. But he had always assumed his father knew that.

That he had not, that it was possible he really had thought Apostolis required *training wheels,* as she did so revoltingly put it, was like a knife in his rib cage.

He blamed her for that, too.

It was turning into a rather long and epic list.

"Everyone knows what is happening here," Apostolis told her, letting his laughter trail off and his eyes blaze right at her, like his fire could melt all her ice. "It's a tale as old as time. A young, avaricious girl seeks an older man to give her a life of comfort and ease. There is only one payment for that, as I think you know. Beauty will always be traded in whatever market that can afford it. No doubt you've spent the last seven years convincing my poor, deluded father that he somehow owed you more than what he'd already given. His name. This life you do not deserve." He made a meal out of a sigh. "Though I do not know why you bothered. No one will ever forget who you really are. No one ever does. A greedy, social climbing trollop who fancies herself a trophy when she is nothing but a sordid little gold digger."

"Do you know what I've noticed?" his bride and nemesis asked, in a deceptively light tone. Apostolis was dimly aware that she was leaning closer to him and that he was leaning closer to her, too. He didn't know when she'd moved, or when he had, only that they were now nearly as close as they had been at that makeshift altar. He could see every furious icicle in her gaze. "Truly wealthy and powerful men take great pleasure in the things that wealth and influence bring them. One of those things being the attention of beautiful women of any social strata."

One of her perfectly shaped brows rose in challenge. "Truly confident men of real authority are never worried about gold digging. Why would they be? They *like* lavishing the women in their lives with the fruits of their labors. And the joy it brings them. For she is the prettiest diamond he could find and oh, does he love polishing her while she gets the chance to truly shine. And do you know who is worried about the apparent scourge of gold diggers traipsing about the planet, looking for unsuspecting marks?"

She nodded sagely, as if he had answered her. "That's right. Tiny little men. With precious little power or authority, who know, deep down, that they'll never measure up."

That she considered him a member of the latter category was obvious.

And for a moment, it was as if Apostolis...*whited out*.

It was as if everything simply...flatlined.

Except not, because he was fully and totally aware of Jolie.

Jolie, that impossible woman, who he had expected would grow brittle to match the void within as the years passed, but she hadn't. He'd expected that gaunt, bird of prey look that so many women in her position adopted as they fought the ravages of time that would eventually get them replaced, but not Jolie.

If anything, she was more beautiful than she'd been on that first wedding day, seven years ago. When she'd stood in a white dress right here in the Andromeda, but that day the sun had been shining and the sea had been so blue it hurt.

And there Jolie had been with her hair the color of the sun, and her eyes a match for the Mediterranean all around her, and only Apostolis seemed to see the truth of who she was.

The sheer avarice in her smile. The calculation in her gaze. The way that she had treated his father as if she was his nurse, not his wife.

I don't expect you to be friends with her, his father had told him with a laugh. *In fact I would prefer you keep your distance, dog that you are. But I do expect you to be polite.*

Apostolis had been certain that *she* could not manage to stay polite. Women like that never could. He had expected her to do what women in her position always did, having secured the older man—as his father had suggested. No doubt they both assumed that the flirtations would start with any younger man who happened by. The coded invitations. The clear and obvious signs that she would be more than willing for some extracurricular with him behind his father's back.

He had spent his father's wedding reception coldly laying out how it would go in his head. How he would expose her and be rid of her.

But those invitations had never come.

To his astonishment, this conceited, manipulative woman had treated him as if *he* was beneath *her*. A charity case she engaged in purely for his father's benefit.

A trial, at best.

For seven years. Without even the slightest deviation.

In fact, it had seemed as if her opinion of him—low to begin with—had only gone lower as time went on.

Even today she was under the impression that *she* was the one doing *him* a favor.

It was an outrage of epic proportions.

Sheer indignation thundered in his veins—and not only because of her temerity.

When he thought about the way he had worked, all of his life, to maintain a relationship with his father, he wanted to…break something. And he knew that while Jolie was an ignominy at best, she was not to blame for the fact that the old man had always loved his work and his women far more than his family.

That he had preferred to bask in the reflected glory of the guests who came and stayed in this hotel, because it gave him some kind of mystique. There were the articles about him, the tycoon who was on a first-name basis with the most powerful and beloved people alive.

The Andromeda is the glittering scene, such articles would claim, *and in the charming epicenter of all that glamour and elegance stands one man. Spyros Adrianakis, the curator of it all.*

Curating that scene had always been more interesting to Spyros than his son. Or his long-suffering wife. Or the baby girl that had not saved his parents' marriage but had instead taken his mother's life and relegated Dioni to her older brother's care. Because he could not trust his sister with the nannies who Spyros had treated like a pool of lovers. All of them auditioning for time in his bed, not the care and maintenance of poor Dioni.

All of this, Apostolis had done his best to forgive. Forgiveness that he was well aware he had never quite achieved.

So he had gotten his father's attention any way he could.

But he was not about to tell this woman, his stepmother *and* wife and *enemy,* such things. He couldn't think of anyone he would trust less with such delicate truths about who he was or what he was about or what this family really was when there was no one about but them.

He studied the enemy in question.

Jolie looked delicate, but she wasn't. He had made a study of her all these years and he knew that the way she presented herself was a lie. The effortlessly willowy form, to easily inhabit this glittering world his father had created, made her look more like one of the grand film stars who flocked to this place, or the high society darlings, than they did themselves.

The greatest lie of all was that she never looked as icy as she truly was. She *looked* like a pure, long shot of a perfect Mediterranean day. All of that golden hair. Those impossible blue eyes. That perfect, symmetrical face, classical cheekbones and the kind of sensual mouth that set pulses to skyrocketing all around.

He knew exactly why his father had chosen her. Aside from the obvious, she was precisely the sort of hostess the Andromeda's extraordinarily particular clientele expected. Demanded, even.

And one thing Apostolis had always known about his father was that as much as Spyros indulged his baser impulses, he never left a mess when it came to the myth of his business. Jolie really was the perfect Lady of the Andromeda, as he had heard her called.

It only made him dislike *his wife* all the more.

Then again, the fact that she'd been forced to marry him could work in his favor. Aside from everything else, it meant that he had ample opportunity to plot and enact the perfect revenge.

His father might not be able to pay for what he'd done, but she could.

And would, Apostolis vowed then, with something like iron in his gut.

Again and again.

"Cat got your tongue?" asked the maddening woman in question, with a certain glee in her voice and all over her lovely face, likely not just because she'd insulted him, but because he'd let her see the insult had found its target.

It was more expression than he'd seen on her face in some time, and he took a dark sort of pleasure in that. Even as he realized with some surprise that while he'd been sorting through the fury and the rage and the fire in him, Alceu and his sister had slipped away, leaving only Apostolis and Jolie in the breakfast room.

How had he failed to notice that?

"It is lucky for you that I am such a small man," he told her then, and stood. Cataloging, as he did, the way her expression changed, and surely not only because he was, in fact, a large man no matter what she thought of him. It told him all manner of interesting things that he filed away for another time. "Or I might be tempted to return the favor."

Jolie's mouth curved in that way it did, that made him think only of sharp blades, polished to shine. And slice. "I wish you would. I can't wait to hear what a rich fantasy life you've been entertaining yourself with all these years."

But revenge was a long game. If the aim was to win.

And he intended to do just that.

Apostolis shook his head. "There will be time enough for that. Five long years."

She stayed where she was, seated with a certain insouciance at the table yet turned in her chair with one arm thrown almost languidly across its back. Yet he found he did not believe her attempt to appear bored by this.

Or him.

"One thousand, eight hundred, and twenty-five days, give or take," she agreed in a quiet voice that was in no way *soft*. "But who's counting?"

And it was a more solemn moment, then, between them. They were looking at each other, for a start. Usually, Apostolis knew, he avoided direct eye contact with this woman like the plague. It was too dangerous—

He wasn't sure he cared to think about why that was.

Apostolis extended his hand, slowly, and did very little to curb the glittering, sharp dislike—that was the only word for it, he was sure—curling through him and no doubt visible on his face.

She wore a very similar expression, ice to his fire.

But she rose.

"Come, my darling wife," Apostolis said in his darkest and most sardonic voice. "And let's start counting the days until we are free of each other."

Jolie smiled again, sharper still. But still she put her hand in his. And hers was smooth, but warm, and he did not wish to acknowledge how he could feel the contact inside him—everywhere—like another thread of that same...*dislike*.

"Until we see, you and I," she said, the blade of that smile honed to a deadly gleam, "who is the most damned."

CHAPTER THREE

THE FUNNY THING about the world ending was that it kept right on going as if her pain didn't matter at all. Her world had ended before, of course. Jolie should have been used to the fact that her pain didn't matter to anyone but herself, and certainly couldn't keep the sun from rising, the tides from turning, or the days from passing as they would.

Her grandparents' deaths had been the first, hardest series of blows. They had raised her after she'd lost her parents when she was two. She often felt profoundly guilty that she couldn't really remember that. She suspected that what she called her memories were actually stories her grandparents had told her about her parents and the pictures they had used to supplement the tales they'd told—of a couple so good it only made sense that they'd been *too* good for the world.

Her grandparents had been Jolie's world. And then, in the course of a bewildering few years, everything had changed.

She had been thirteen when her grandmother died. She and her grandfather had mourned together until he had decided that regular school was not enough for his only grandchild, and so had sent her off to finishing school when she was barely seventeen. So that she, like her grandmother before her, could learn how to be a woman of consequence.

I thought finishing schools turned girls into women who married consequence rather than becoming it themselves, she had complained.

Her grandfather had laughed, his kind eyes crinkling in the corners. *Perhaps. But married to whom, pray? One thing this particular school will do,* mon rayon de soleil, *is teach you how to* think.

He had maintained that the school would be the making of her until she had gone to take her place there. And within a few months he had succumbed to pneumonia and was gone, too.

That would have been quite enough change. But her grandfather had possessed what he liked to call *a bit of a buffer against the world's trials.* What it was, in fact, was a small fortune. When he died he left the whole of it to Jolie.

But because she was only seventeen, there were strings attached.

And those strings were her aunt and uncle. The court had appointed them trustees. They had oozed sincerity and warmth, despite the fact that her aunt—her mother's sister—had been estranged from the family for as long as Jolie could remember.

Jolie had believed they were who they said they were. Concerned relatives who wanted only to help their poor niece after a loss so devastating it must surely smooth over any past troubles.

She had not been so naïve since.

Jolie realized with a start that she'd been more or less sleepwalking through the hotel, thinking about all the various *ends of the world* she'd lived through thus far. She blinked, shaking her head as she looked around, hoping that none of the staff—or more importantly, Apostolis—had seen her in such a distracted state.

Today was a changeover day, a week since her doomed wedding. Their last famous guest had left the day before, and as the Hotel Andromeda did not enforce checkout times on the clientele they treated like family, the guest in question and his expansive selection of acolytes had not chosen to leave until so late last night it was actually this morning.

This was why they always did their best to put a day of padding in between. There was no telling when a guest would ignore their checkout day altogether and have to be gently and politely—but never directly—encouraged to move on before the next guest arrived.

They had the whole day today, which was less time than it seemed after a tornado of fame and money went through the place. Their handpicked, miracle-working staff was already deep into the process of turning the entire old house inside out and upside down so that when the next set of guests arrived it would be as if the hotel had been waiting for them since their last visit. This time it was a family that would stay for a month, and liked the Andromeda to feel as if it was their home.

With occasional effortlessly glamorous drinks with the owner, of course. Since Spyros's death, the guests had liked to get together in the evenings and reminisce about the old man. Jolie only hoped that she could manage to keep her cool, as expected, now that she would not be reminiscing with the guests on her own.

This was not easy because Apostolis was not easy. A funny thing to say about a man who made such a point of acting lazy whenever possible, but it was true. She had imagined they might simply go about their business and ignore each other as much as possible, but he was always poking at her. Always seething in her direction, right there under the surface where, apparently, only she could see it.

He really is the most gloriously charming man alive, isn't he? one of the former guest's acolytes had sighed at Jolie only a few days ago, her eyes dancing with stars and focused on Apostolis. *I don't know how you can* bear *being around him all the time.*

This after Apostolis had managed to quietly insult her in a variety of ways throughout the evening, but apparently at a frequency only she could hear.

It is a great trial, she had replied. Truthfully. Though she'd had to smile enigmatically while she said it to make it seem as if she meant the opposite.

There was something so unfair about it, she thought now. That despite their mutual loathing—or perhaps because of it—she and Apostolis were the only ones who could see each other clearly.

She had been doing a walk-through of all the floral arrangements before she'd been sidetracked into unpleasant memories, one of her managerial tasks that she liked best. She had built a relationship these past seven years with all the florists in the village and used each of them all in a rotation, depending on the guest in question. The Andromeda liked to present each guest with a floral theme, a *flowerscape*, as Jolie and Dioni liked to call it.

Spyros had praised her for her attention to such things, and his only compliments were always about the business. Like the scent profiles she curated, a comprehensive collection of scents that worked with each other, never against, and only completed the floral arrangements. It was not as simple as one might think.

Jolie carried on moving through the old mansion, in and out of the rooms that could all be locked up into separate suites but were left open and welcoming today, anticipating that the family group would wish to move freely. The rooms were large and graceful, and let in the light. Since that storm that had soaked her wedding right through, the best wedding gift she'd received, the island had returned to form. Everything was gold and blue, with bright flowers bursting into vibrant color everywhere. Inside the hotel, the palette was more understated, allowing the unmistakable beauty of the landscape and the sea to shine.

She loved this place. This grand and glorious old hotel. It had been one of the unexpected gifts of this path she'd been forced to take.

After checking out all the arrangements on this floor, she wandered into the library to assess the flowers that stood on the table directly beneath the vaulted skylight, one of Spyros's additions to the house. The flowers were appropriately theatrical, but she found herself drifting over to the shelves stuffed with books, never artificially arranged.

It had been the first room she'd found herself gravitating to when Spyros had brought her here. She supposed that it reminded her of her grandfather's study in the chateau outside Lausanne with its view of Lake Geneva and the Alps, filled with books, dear old rugs, and funny little items of art and interest that her grandparents had collected from all over the world.

The chateau, too, was gone now. What had been meant to be her birthright had been sold right out from under her.

Jolie had been almost done with finishing school before she understood what was happening. She had never cared much about her grandfather's will, or the fortune she had hardly been able to comprehend was to be hers. Because she hadn't had to worry about it, she understood now. And by the time she realized that she was no longer protected, it was too late.

The pain of that never quite left her.

She sank down in one of the comfortable seats in the Hotel Andromeda library and blew out a breath, remembering that terrible day when she'd finally fully understood the truth of things. She'd been nineteen and she'd thought that she was misunderstanding something, that was all. She had tried to use one of the cards her grandfather had always designated for her use, only to have it declined. That had sent her on what should not have been an arduous journey to locate her aunt and uncle, who were not living where they'd told her they were.

Jolie had tracked them down at the chateau. The chateau that did not resemble the home she had left that fall because they'd stripped it clean. And were in the process of selling it off, piece by piece.

I... I don't understand, Jolie had managed to say, close to tears as she stood in the entry hall, looking around at bare walls and empty rooms beyond in shock.

I deserve it, after the way they treated me, her aunt had said, an ugly triumph making her face twist. *And I've taken it.*

And you're welcome to do something about it, if you like, her uncle had chimed in with an unpleasant laugh. *But by the time you do, it will all be gone.*

Their daughter Mathilde had been sitting on the steps behind them, her eyes wide. And Jolie had seen that same frightened awareness in her cousin that she knew must be written all over her. It had made her heart lurch inside her chest.

But... But that's not right, Jolie had sputtered.

Because back then, she'd still imagined that something like honor, or truth, or *what was right* mattered to anyone.

The truth was, her aunt and uncle had taught her a series of very valuable lessons.

At first, Jolie had felt helpless. They had sacked her home, pillaged her future, and taken everything that had meant anything to her. Oh, she knew that they thought she was upset about the money. But she'd never had any comprehension of that. Of what it meant.

What they had thrown away were her memories.

All those pictures. All those objects, softened by all

the fingers she'd loved that had touched them. Paintings that were not just art to her, but windows into the marvelous stories of their travels.

All of it, gone.

But what is to become of me? she had asked them.

Her aunt had laughed and laughed.

Her uncle had snarled. *That school of yours should set you up just fine to marry one of the rich men always hovering about. That's what Mathilde will do when it's her time, and she won't be breathing in your rarefied air, will she?*

Again, the cousins had gazed at each other, each entirely too clear about what he must mean. Though, looking back, Jolie knew that she—at the least—had truly had no idea.

Some of us have to make do, her aunt had said with another unpleasant laugh. *You will find out, little mademoiselle. Soon enough, I should think.*

Sitting in an armchair in the library of the very rich man she'd gone ahead and married, Jolie found herself feeling something like rueful.

Because, of course, she had not wanted to marry anyone. She had vowed that she would do no such thing.

But over the course of her last year at school, her stark financial situation had been made clear to her. Her grandfather had paid her tuition in advance, but she was otherwise penniless. She had confessed everything to the headmistress one cold winter's day, and the older woman had listened with sympathy.

And then had fixed Jolie with a gimlet eye. *I am not*

saying that your horrid relatives are right, in any regard, she had said. *But the fact remains that while this institution has been happily responsible for the education of many strong and powerful women in their own right, from politicians to activists to philanthropists of all kinds, its original purpose was to do all of those things but in the form—*

Of a wife, Jolie had said hollowly.

Not just any wife, the headmistress had replied, a stern sort of glint in her gaze. *This institution does not create trophies. It assures triumphs.*

What she did not ask, but what had hung there between them anyway, was, *Do you have any better ideas?*

And so, when her classmate's very old father had paid her close attention that spring, she'd accepted it. She had returned it, cautiously. And had gotten far more than financial security out of the bargain.

She had become instantly famous, everywhere, the moment her name was linked to *the* Spyros Adrianakis. Having not heard from her aunt and uncle in a couple of years by then, they had found a way to get in touch with her again once they heard the news. Perhaps unsurprisingly—though it made Jolie sad and bitter in turn—they had already run through the fortune they'd stolen.

Yet by that time, married to Spyros and living at the hotel in the company of so many different kinds of powerful people, Jolie was a far cry from the naïve girl they had taken advantage of years before.

The only reason she hadn't cut them off without a

second thought was Mathilde. Who was, by that point, all of thirteen. And deserved her parents as little as Jolie had.

She was afraid she knew exactly what kind of things they might do with a pretty girl like Mathilde.

How could she live with herself if she let them? When she could do something to stop them? She couldn't. She just *couldn't.*

So she'd done the only thing she could. She'd struck a bargain.

And she'd been paying for it ever since.

Still, it was good to remind herself that she hadn't simply *ended up* here, she told herself now, gazing at the bookshelves before her that fairly *ached* with all the books they held. Even this marriage she found herself in now was a choice she'd made. Because, after all, a lack of *good* choices wasn't the same thing as a lack of choices.

You survived this far, she reminded herself. *You'll survive a little longer.*

Maybe then, when all the surviving was done, maybe she would give *living* a try.

But first there were flower arrangements and incoming guests. Bookkeeping and bills. Myths to embody and legends to keep afloat. Yet just as she was preparing to get back to her to-do list, something changed.

There was a disturbance in the air. And it seemed to be connected directly to her nervous system, or perhaps it was simply in her bones.

It was a winnowing. A tightening. A sudden shift.

Jolie was completely unsurprised to look up and find Apostolis there in the door to the library.

"Working hard I see," he said with his usual censure. When they were alone, he didn't bother to dress it up in a charming, playboyish smile. And she could have disabused him of the notion that she was lazy. That all she did here was lounge about, avoiding work. But that might indicate that she cared what he thought of her.

She couldn't have that.

Jolie went even more languid in the chair. She made her hand wave a work of artful ennui. "I am the trophy wife, remember? Why should I work?"

She had the distinct pleasure of watching those distractingly sensual lips of his firm, then press into a tight line. Maybe one day she would find herself adult enough—mature enough—to keep from feeling joy when she jabbed at this man. One day she would find her way to blessed indifference.

But that was not today.

"I am not my father," he told her, with that seething note in his dark voice.

He drew closer and everything in her urged her to stand up, to face off with him. To do what she could to at least stand tall before him—which was not tall enough, but certainly put her more the level of his face than she was now.

But she didn't.

Jolie lounged in that chair, giving every impression that she was exactly the sort of spoiled little party girl he thought she was.

"Is this an identity crisis?" she asked as he stalked

closer. "If so, my suggestion for you is to seek therapy. Daddy issues can be so pernicious."

He didn't respond to that directly, but she did enjoy the slight flare of his nostrils, and the way the muscles in his jaw clenched tight. It was the little things.

"I understand that you might think that nothing will be expected of you. I imagine that's how your life has gone up to this point. But I have no intention of carrying you along like dead weight. You will work—"

"Or what?" she asked mildly. "For one thing, we're stuck with each other and no one put you in charge. For another, what exactly do you know about the business of running the Hotel Andromeda, Apostolis?"

"Anything my father could do, I'm quite certain I can do better."

She made herself laugh, though that hard look he had trained on her made it more difficult than it should have been. "And again I say…daddy issues."

"It is nothing to do with *daddy issues*." And the way he said those words made her think that the very taste of them in his mouth was sour. She liked that, too. "It is a simple fact that he was an old man. His attention to detail has slipped, to put it mildly." He shook his head at her, doing nothing at all to hide his distaste. "As his wife, I would expect you to have noticed that."

This time she laughed to cover her own surprise. "You'd be surprised the sorts of things I know about the men I've married."

She made that sound airy, as if she was just talking rubbish to annoy him. Inside, however, she was more than a little shaken.

Because in the past, she would have asserted with total confidence that Apostolis did not know a single thing about his father. His visits, spaced out as they were, were always all about him. There was no possible way he could know the first thing about Spyros as a man. Or the challenges the old man had faced in his waning years.

And she wondered if she would have felt this surge of something like loyalty to his father if she had been married to anyone but him. If it was actual loyalty to Spyros she felt—when she had never felt any such thing before—or a simple, possibly childish desire not to give Apostolis *anything*.

Not even the things she knew about his father that he didn't.

"I am sure that you are a great talent and know many, many fascinating things," Apostolis said then, his meaning clear as he swept a gaze over the length of her body. "None of them, I think, useful in the running of a hotel."

"Because you are the expert, is that it?"

Jolie regarded him steadily, because she'd found that it made him uncomfortable when she did so and today was no different. She could see the way he lowered his chin. The way his jaw tightened even further, almost certainly risking his famous smile.

And then, a far more telltale sign, he crossed his arms.

That felt like a win, so she smiled. "I think you'll find, Apostolis, that spending many a debaucherous evening in whatever hotel crosses your drunken path is not *quite* the same thing as running one. And even if it was, the kind of hotels that cater to your sort of character are very different from the Andromeda."

"I'll thank you to remember that the Andromeda is my birthright, not yours."

"Birthrights are funny things," she said, and there was, regrettably, more emotion in her voice than she might have wished in his presence. She hoped he would think it was temper. "They seem like rocks, do they not? Slabs of immovable granite that one can stand upon. Until they're gone."

His gaze was a wildfire. "Is that a threat?"

It hadn't been. It had been a bit of foolishness and wistfulness, nothing more—but then her breath caught because he moved forward. And before she could do anything at all, he was leaning over, bracing himself with a hand on each arm of her chair.

Caging her in.

He wasn't touching her. She knew he wasn't touching her—

And yet her body exploded into a riot of sensation, as if he was.

She felt hemmed in on all sides, as if she was trapped in his closed fist, but there was something far worse than that—and it was that she felt *precious* there.

As if that fist closed around her was protecting her, not confining her at all.

And it didn't help that the way he was leaning over her meant he'd put his face entirely too close to hers.

So that she was forced, entirely against her will, to

CAITLIN CREWS 55

remember in excruciating detail that final moment of their wedding ceremony.

You may kiss the bride, the priest had intoned.

She and Apostolis had stared each other down, with varying looks of horror and distaste.

But she was no coward, so she had stepped forward and tipped her head back, daring him. And he had accepted that dare at once, moving in and sliding a hand around to the small of her back, which had been…unpleasant.

Wildly, riotously unpleasant, she had assured herself.

And then—never closing his eyes, which she knew because she never closed hers—they had glared at each other while their lips brushed.

Jolie had instantly repressed that moment, until now.

Because now he was much too close, *again.* With that archangel's face of his and that look of burning distaste—for that was surely what it was—in his too-hot gaze.

She remembered the glare, the brush of their lips.

And the immediate, almost terrifying brush fire that had soared through her in its wake.

Here, in this chair in the library where she doubted she would find peace again, she could feel the lick of those same flames.

"Why are you worried about threats?" she had the presence of mind to ask him. "Do you feel threatened, husband?"

"The nature of a threat is mutable. Is it a promise? A suggestion?"

She lifted her chin, feeling defiant and not entirely understanding why. "I did not realize you were such a philosopher."

"And I thought you were an expert on your many husbands," he retorted in that sardonic tone of his. Almost chiding her. "But then again, you clearly enjoyed a certain...intimacy with my father that you and I do not share."

Something about that prickled in her, some mix of indignation and shame and not a little bit of temper, besides.

"Are you talking about sex?" She laughed into the breath of space between them. "And here I was beginning to think that the modern-day whore of Babylon himself had come over all missish. What would all your favorite tabloids say if they knew?"

"I suppose it would take one whore to know another," he replied, too easily. Too smoothly.

Because it took her one whole breath and half of another to understand that what he had really done was slide a knife in deep between her ribs.

The pain of it was so intense and so surprising, because it was so unfair, that she felt her eyes go bright.

"Don't think that I don't understand where all of this animosity is coming from," she told him, using whatever blades she had to hand, and hurling them as hard as she could. "It must be so confusing for you to finally meet a woman immune to what I think I've heard called your *charm*."

"Immunity would look like indifference, my darling

wife," he said, so softly. Too softly. "And you are many things in my presence, but indifferent? I think not."

"By that metric, I suspect you must be half in love with me," she said, lightly enough, yet sharp enough, to leave scars.

But before scars, there was blood, and they both knew she'd drawn his.

It seemed to shimmer there, in the air between them.

"Should we test that?" he asked, a scant breath that took the shape of words.

Even if she'd understood what he was asking, she would not have backed down from the challenge. Any challenge.

But she didn't understand.

When he leaned in even closer, then set his mouth to hers, she was wholly unprepared. And there was nothing for it but to burn.

She had never confused Apostolis with his father. For a host of reasons, none of which she intended to share with him, now or ever.

But if she had, this would have scorched any stray wisp of a memory of Spyros from her brain.

His hands stayed on the arms of the chair. The only place they touched at all was at the mouth. The lips. The tongues.

But that was more than enough.

Because he did not simply brush his lips over hers and call it a kiss.

That there was any resemblance between that first kiss and this *incineration*, that they should both share the same name, was almost laughable.

Because what he did was lick his way into her mouth, flooding her with the most intense sensation she had ever felt. Then, as if that would not have knocked her on her bottom had she not already been sitting, he angled his jaw.

He made it all…hotter. Deeper. And decidedly worse.

So much worse.

Distractingly, outrageously, irresistibly worse.

And this kiss that was so much more than a kiss went on and on.

It was a feast—a banquet of sensation—and she found herself responding against her will. There was nothing she could do but follow that fire, chasing that sensation any way she could.

Until it was as if their tongues were engaged in the same sweet, slick dance. As if they were both trying to burn each other alive, but this was not a flame that either one of them could control.

Nor should you want to, something in her whispered.

It was too bright, too bold. It grew too big, too fast.

And maybe she already knew that he would leave her in cinders.

Jolie pulled away and she felt a kind of triumph that she could. But it was a close call. And she only realized, then, that it hadn't occurred to her to keep her eyes open in protest the way she had before.

Something that was obvious to her because now, she could see him.

She could see the look on his face, intent and too hot to look at directly, though she did.

And let it sear straight through her.

Jolie decided she had only one play here. Only one chance to win this battle despite losing herself—and clearly losing her head—with this kiss she should never have allowed.

She'd know better now. She'd be more careful.

He had weapons she hadn't dared imagine, but now she would.

First, though, she had to win. Or more accurately— he had to lose.

So she sat forward and slid her hand over his jaw, the better to smile at him as if she meant it.

"Tell me, husband," she said quietly. Almost sweetly, her gaze steady on his. "Does that feel like threat enough to you now?"

And it was worth it to watch his face shutter, instantly. To watch him straighten and move back as if she had kicked him in the gut.

It was worth it to smile in the face of the look of pure loathing he threw her way, and keep smiling as he wheeled around and strode from the room.

And only then, only when she was alone, did Jolie cover her face with her shaking hands and do the best she could to keep from falling apart.

CHAPTER FOUR

THAT HE WAS a cursed man living a cursed life became, over the next weeks, a foregone conclusion even if it was not a surprise. Apostolis had spent the bulk of his life sorting out his own personal tragedies and attempting to come to terms with them.

Why should his marriage be any different?

"The scandal of your wedding has saturated the culture to such an extent that it has even reached me," his friend Alceu told him on one of their calls one day.

"I have always been a scandal," Apostolis said idly. "Why shouldn't I compound it now? Maybe I'll keep going. At what point does a scandal become too much scandal?"

"When there is any hint of scandal at all," Alceu said in his usual repressive tones. "I suspect, my friend, that there is no hope for the man who made his stepmother his wife."

"But was there ever any hope for me?" Apostolis asked in the same musing sort of way.

He could hear his friend's sigh. "I have never had any."

And yet, somehow, the conversation left him in a more hopeful frame of mind than he'd been in before.

He moved to the window of the hotel's executive offices, such as they were, that were located on the bottom floor of the carriage house that had sat beside the Andromeda for almost as long as the hotel itself. Longer, according to some accounts. The grounds of the hotel lounged about along the cliff top and in addition to the mansion itself, there were a number of outbuildings. Maintenance sheds, garages, stables, and so on. There was also the carriage house, which was not only the offices but also his own quarters since he'd been about ten. And the back house, as it was called even though it was technically to the side of the hotel, where he had lived as a small boy, his sister still lived, and his father had lived with Jolie.

Apostolis found that as time went on, he grew less and less sanguine about the fact that Jolie had been his father's wife first.

He found it harder and harder to accept that reality.

Yet he could still taste her in his mouth. She had invaded his sleep.

This was a new development.

He loathed it.

In his dreams, that scene in the library did not end where it had that day. In his dreams he lifted her up into his arms and took her down onto the library floor. He stripped her of those clothes she wore—all that casual, offhanded elegance, no match for the real Jolie there beneath the things she wore.

In his dreams, he tasted every centimeter of her flesh and drank deep between her thighs until he had her moaning and writhing in his grip.

And his dreams never stopped there, either.

Every night, his dreams presented him with another way to slake this wildfire in him. Every night, he found that there was no balance to his imagination and no brakes besides. Not when it came to her.

As if, all along, he had not so much hated her for all the appropriate reasons, but desired her—

But no. He could not accept it.

And it made interacting with her in the light of day a challenge.

She would stand before him throwing all her usual barbs and all he would think about was how deep inside of her he'd been in last night's deliriously hot dream. How she had arched her back and pressed her breast to his mouth. How she tossed back her head in abandon when she rode him hard and deep.

Are you listening to me? she had asked a bit sharply this morning.

But he'd studied the way her gaze widened as he looked at her.

And he'd wondered if she'd had an idea what he was thinking about without him having to say a word.

Of course I wasn't listening, he had told her, after a fraught moment or two passed. *I never listen when you're insulting me. Which means, my darling wife, it's as if we live in this lovely spot in perfect silence. Nothing but the waves and the wind.*

He had been proud of that.

She had looked rather more incandescent, though she had walked away before he could see if she might truly lose her cool at last.

Apostolis was enjoying imagining how else that moment might have ended when he heard a knock at the office door. He turned, aware that something in him leaped a bit at the notion it might be his wife.

But he tempered that reaction almost as soon as he had it. Because, for one thing, Jolie rarely knocked on any door at the Andromeda, since she was half owner of the hotel. As she liked to remind him daily. And for another, that was not the reaction he should have been having where she was concerned.

And besides, it was Dioni. He smiled at his sister with genuine warmth. "You don't have to knock, Dioni *mou*. This is your house as well as mine."

Dioni inched into the room and he felt the same swell of affection and bafflement that he always did at the sight of his sister. Their mother had been exquisite. A woman of such impeccable taste and glorious style that, to this day, he had never met a person who'd known her who didn't mention those things immediately.

And yet this was her daughter. His sister, the jewel of the house of Adrianakis, who scurried about like some kind of woodland animal.

"Well, that's a lovely thing to say but it's not really my house, is it?" If someone else had said something like that, it would have been a complaint. But this was Dioni. He had never heard her complain. Because a complaint was part and parcel of some kind of darkness, and as far as he was aware, she had never known even the faintest shadow. "It's your house. And Jolie's house. Father did not leave me anything."

"He left you me," he corrected her, surprised when perhaps he should not have been. "And I will see to it, as he did, that you will never want for a thing."

His sister made her way further into the office and sat in the chair before his desk. And he looked at her, struck by the notion that he hadn't really looked at her closely in some time. Not since the wedding, which was weeks ago now. She looked...

Different, he thought. It took him a moment to realize why. Her hair wasn't falling down all around her. He could see no stains or tears in her clothing.

He frowned. "Are you all right?"

He could have sworn that she flinched then, though she hid it in the next moment. But then again, this was his sister who had never hidden anything from him. He was certain that he must have been mistaken.

She frowned at him. "Why would I be different? What do you mean?"

Apostolis had always thought that his role as her brother was not to mention her appearance, which he knew everyone else harped on. Or worse, tried to *help her,* which she always suffered with good grace only to turn up disheveled just the same.

He had always found it charming.

"Only you can tell you're different or not, little mouse," he said, and again, she did something out of the ordinary. It was as if she bristled, but then caught herself.

"I finally decided what I want to do with my life," she said. And he thought she sounded unlike herself, but he was not going to tell her that. "I've decided that I'm going to pack up and move to America."

"America?" He didn't laugh. He could sense she wouldn't like it. "America is a large place, Dioni. Have you picked a specific *part* of the country?"

"I will." She frowned at him again, and more deeply this time. "What I need you to do is be okay with it when I go."

And maybe he was a worse brother than he'd ever imagined, because he didn't think about anything at all in that moment except having the privacy to handle Jolie the way he wanted. At last.

Because he thought he finally knew how. It came to him in a blinding flash the moment he understood that he'd been wanting this privacy all along. He and Jolie had settled into their marriage, such as it was, by playing their roles in public—but continuing to live in their separate quarters. This arrangement had not seemed to worry his sister at all, or cause her to question their marriage in any way. *Seeming happiness* could involve separate beds, as far as the innocent Dioni knew.

Yet *happy* was not how Apostolis would describe himself. Or his marriage.

He'd been dreaming this solution all along. It might be inconvenient to find he desired his stepmother in this way, and he chose not to question why it felt more like a long overdue *recognition* than some new bolt from the blue, but he could use it. He *would* use it.

Because he finally had the weapon he needed to win this war decisively.

But here and now, he had to force himself to concentrate.

"First of all, you can go wherever you like, for as long as you like, and do whatever takes your fancy." The Dioni he knew would have smiled brightly at that and started chattering on merrily about the great many projects that were already lighting up her mind. But today, his sister only looked back at him, but with that steady frown in place. He was tempted to think she was making him the slightest bit uneasy, but of course she wasn't. This was *Dioni*. And he did not get *uneasy*. "If you wish to go to America, there is no need for mystery. I have properties in New York, Miami, and Los Angeles. And, of course, Hawaii."

That got a reaction from his sister. She blinked. "You do?"

"Don't tell anyone," he told her, with a grin. "It would ruin my image. The world prefers to consider me the grand waste of space our father did. And perhaps I am. But either way, I also have a robust real estate portfolio."

He smiled blandly as his sister came close to gaping at him and wondered how she would react if she knew how he actually spent his time, or that Alceu was his partner in those far more low-profile activities. "Remember, Dioni. It's a secret."

"I think I'd like to go to New York City," she said after a moment, then turned her frown toward the windows. "I don't want any more beaches. I want concrete canyons and furious impatience wherever I turn."

Somehow Apostolis thought that she would find the brownstone he owned in Manhattan's West Village neighborhood, complete with its own garden, a little less *impatient* than the rest of the city. But she could discover that for herself. "Are you sure?" he asked. When she nodded, he carried on. "Then only say the word, and we will have—"

"I am ready for a change," his sister said, cutting him off. "Now."

Her asserting anything so strongly was so unusual that he actually gazed back at her in something approximating shock.

"All right then. You can leave tonight if you like."

"Wonderful," Dioni replied, but even then she didn't sound like her normally cheerful self. There was something brittle about her. He didn't like it.

But if she didn't want to tell him, he didn't see how he could force her. And in any case, he knew from his own experience across many brooding years that while the geographic cure never quite lived up to its name, sometimes, a Band-Aid in place of an *actual cure* could do the trick just the same.

His sister deserved to find these things out for herself.

Everything happened swiftly, then. He called to have the plane readied. She went off to oversee the packing of her things—or perhaps, for all he knew, she was already packed.

And that evening, only a few hours after Dioni had

come to speak to him in the office, Apostolis and Jolie stood out on the tarmac on the other side of the island—together—and said their goodbyes.

"I will miss you," he told his sister fiercely when she hugged him.

"Really do miss me, then," she replied, but she was smiling. "Don't get weird and spy on me."

"I would never dream of it," he lied, and made a mental note to pare back the security detail he'd planned to keep in her vicinity.

He watched as Dioni hugged Jolie and thought it seemed longer and harder for someone merely taking off on a new adventure. Particularly when she was late to that game. Many people did such things when they were younger, with their gap years and their regrettable twenties.

But he was a terrible brother, clearly, because the only thing he could truly concentrate on was the fact there was the hotel and its guests waiting for them—but other than that, only and him and Jolie on the property. Staff quarters were further down from the cliff, giving them a bit of a break from the hotel when they weren't on duty.

Members of the family had no breaks. And now his wife had nowhere to hide.

And maybe the anticipation of that was humming in him a little too brightly, because Jolie looked at him in askance when he started the sleek Range Rover and aimed it at the coastal road that hugged the coastline, then meandered along the length of the island to the Andromeda.

Especially when he drove a bit too fast.

"I have never known Dioni to be so…" Jolie began.

"Independent?" he offered. "Secretive? Strange?"

"Solitary," Jolie replied.

Perhaps a little repressively.

But he found that whatever else he might object to in this woman, her friendship with his sister was something that could only win his approval. Especially when Jolie possessed precisely that sort of effortless elegance that his sister lacked so profoundly.

Others had been cruel. He had realized in his time here that Jolie, no matter her many other faults, was never anything but kind to Dioni.

It was tempting to imagine there were whole other parts of her he could not see—

But he cast that worrying thought aside.

She was sitting in the passenger seat, so there was only so far away from him she could be based on the dimensions of the vehicle. Yet Jolie, somehow, managed to make it seem as if she'd put an extra ice floe or two between them.

He took satisfaction, tremendous satisfaction, in knowing that that was something she was not going to be able to do for much longer.

Not with any success.

"Change is good," he said, thinking of the various ways he knew to melt ice. "There were whole years of my life where change was the only constant. It's time Dioni discovered who she is and who she wants to be, away from the shadow of all this."

"And do you think you managed to do it?" came Jolie's silky, too serene tone, though her gaze was trained out the window. "Do you think you successfully removed yourself from any pesky shadows or do you worry that all you've done is run about to no avail, only to end up where you started?"

Normally he would have shot right back. But there were all those dreams in the night. Every night. There were all the ways he'd already had her when he had barely touched her. There was that kiss and the repercussions of that, and the way it echoed through him, even now. As if it was simply a part of him.

That wasn't anything new. What was new was that he knew that everything between them was about to change.

And, perhaps, the fact that beneath her icy exterior, she cared for the sister he had always protected to the best of his ability.

It allowed him to answer with more candor than he might have otherwise. "I never considered myself to be in my father's shadow. Quite the opposite. He would have had to be present in my life in some meaningful way for me to consider myself overshadowed by him."

"Some would say that his legend alone does that work," Jolie murmured.

"His legend has never meant much to me. I have read about it in magazines, like anyone else. In fawning articles that carry on about the secret lifestyles of famous men and the places they like to habit, like the Andromeda. I'm fully aware of the mystique. Of the hotel *and* the man." Apostolis shrugged. "But for me it was my childhood home. A mother who tried to please her husband, and then died. And a father who was always too busy chasing women—before and after he was widower—and courting the attention of celebrities to pay any attention at all to any of us. I like my family's legacy. I want to continue it, as my mother would have wanted. The hotel and its legend is important to me. My father's personal legend I could do without."

He felt her turn to look at him then, and he congratulated himself, because surely allowing her to imagine him vulnerable was the greatest weapon he'd employed yet.

But he found himself glancing over just the same, to gauge the particular color of her Mediterranean blue eyes.

"I was orphaned when I was two," she told him after a long curve in the road brought them past one of the villages, white-walled and blue-shuttered. "I never really knew my parents, so I can't say that I mourned them, specifically. But I have to imagine that having parents and yet not having them must in some ways be harder than not having them at all. I never wondered if our relationship could improve. I never tortured myself with fantasies about the way that things could be different between us. And when I imagine them, it's the fantasy versions of them my grandparents created for me, as bedtime stories. I never got to know their flaws and foibles. I never had to measure myself against them and see where they came up lacking, or I did." She let out a long, low breath. "So I don't envy you, Apostolis. Whether you call it a shadow or not, it must be a weight all the same."

He had pulled up to the hotel and now he navigated the car to a stop in front of the carriage house. When he did, he looked over at her and could not tell if the weight he felt inside him was that shadow she'd spoke of, or if it was that unexpected mix of compassion and grief that she'd shared with him.

Apostolis was in knots, but Jolie wasn't even looking at him. She looked almost supernaturally composed, her head angled away from him, her gaze out toward the sea.

But he had the strangest urge to reach over and trace the line of her jaw, because it looked sharper than usual, as if she'd set it against the same memories she'd just shared with him.

He stopped himself right there. Whatever game she was playing here, whatever battle tactic this was, he would be a fool to fall for it.

She turned to look at him then, and suddenly he could feel shadows everywhere, as if they were both soaked in them. Or maybe it was the ghosts of what could have been. Of what might have been.

If he had met her somewhere other than on his father's arm, years ago.

He had never felt anything like it, that sudden pang of loss. And never so keenly, the ache of it so intense it made his bones hurt.

And though he couldn't read anything on her face, he somehow thought that what he saw there was a thread of true vulnerability. Or something more akin to openness.

Whatever it was, it had no place between them.

This *hurt* had no place in this war.

And she must have told herself the same thing, he thought, because she was the one who spoke first. She was the one who broke this odd moment in half.

"We will have to hurry," she said, in a brisk sort of voice, as if they hadn't been talking about *shadows* only moments before.

"Hurry?" he repeated, feeling…off-kilter.

It was not a sensation he enjoyed. And he would consider it one more mark against her, he decided. One more offense she would need to answer for, in the most delectable way possible.

"It is almost time for cocktails on the terrace, which most guests demand," she told him, that edge in her voice back as if it had never been gone. "This is the sort of thing that the proprietor of the Andromeda must never forget, Apostolis. It is one among many tiny little details that must be welded to your bones, as much a part of you as breath. Our last guest and his entourage preferred their own company, but that is unusual. Normally, not only must you follow the schedule every day in and day out, you must make certain that our guests feel as if there is no schedule at all. As if it is merely spontaneous, the joy we find in their presence, and so we celebrate it with a bottle of something lovely beneath the stars of an evening."

He wasn't sure what moved in him then. Was it a dark thread of laughter? Or was he more inclined to… shout?

"I don't know why I am always so astonished that every last part of you is a work of theater," he found himself saying, his voice low and urgent in a way that might have alarmed him, but it was better than shouting. And he was too busy trying to work out that look on her face. Why couldn't he categorize it?

"I can tell that you mean that to be an insult." Jolie rolled her eyes as if to say, *and a weak one at that.* "But I'm not insulted. On the contrary, you could not have complimented me more if you tried. Your father made it clear that he wanted me to inhabit the role of the iconic hostess here. Unknowable, yet everyone's confidante, and so on. I'm glad to know I've done that."

She didn't wait to see his reaction to that, the way any other woman he'd ever known would have. And always had. Instead, she opened up her door and climbed out of the Range Rover as if she'd finished with this conversation.

Or perhaps with him altogether.

That wasn't the reason he found himself following suit, and quickly, he assured himself. He was simply exiting the vehicle.

And he found her again in the middle of the drive, the sea at her back, the olive trees on the hill, and standing there above them, the Andromeda. Keeping a silent, watchful eye on everything, as always.

Only a fool would complicate the situation by touching her, but Apostolis did it anyway. He took her wrist in his hand and found himself staring down at that point of contact. It took him too long to lift his eyes to hers again, and when he did he found her regarding him.

Again with a look he could not name in her gaze.

"Careful," she said, almost too quietly. "Just because you can't see anyone doesn't mean we're not in public. That's one of the first things your father taught me."

"I suppose I'm delighted to hear that he was able to impart his version of wisdom to someone," Apostolis gritted out.

Something not quite a smile moved over her face. "Says the man who claims there's no shadow over his life, when he is little more than an eclipsed moon trying too hard to act the part of the sun."

It felt like a knife to the gut.

He told himself it was comforting, somehow. A return to form.

"I thought I'd lost you somewhere on the coastal road," he said, not breaking eye contact. "Unexpected vulnerability? A perfectly civil conversation, no less? I hardly knew you at all."

She pulled her hand from his grasp, both of them aware that he could have held onto her if he'd wanted to. And he took an atavistic pleasure in the way her own hand went to cover the place he'd touched her, as if she needed to soothe the sensation.

Or hold it close.

"Dioni is a good friend of mine," she told him with that quiet dignity that he knew was meant to make him feel small. He told himself it didn't work. "I'm going to miss her. She has…always been here. As long as I've been here, anyway. It will feel empty without her."

"It won't for long," he told her then, deciding in that

instant that telling her now actually made it harder on her. He wasn't pulling a punch, he was making sure it landed harder. That it reverberated more fully.

He certainly wasn't attempting to make her *feel better*.

A faint frown sketched itself between her brows. "I can only imagine what that's supposed to mean."

"No need to imagine, my dear and darling wife," he drawled, enjoying the thick weight of that satisfaction deep within him. "It's not a secret. I've had all your things moved into the carriage house. Isn't it wonderful? We will finally live together as man and wife."

And then he left her there, sputtering on the drive, and went to play the role of *iconic host* himself.

Because she might have won some points, reminding him that his role here had more to do with the longevity of the hotel and less to do with his childhood here. And that much of that longevity relied upon the kind of legend he built in the wake of his father's.

He hoped he was man enough to take good advice when he heard it, no matter the source, because he'd always prided himself on that before.

Because he was here to make sure that the legend his mother had given her life to could sustain itself despite Spyros. That it could carry on, long after Spyros was entirely forgotten—the most fitting end to the story of his narcissistic father he could imagine.

And later tonight, after committing himself to a role he'd once vowed he would never take—*Because I want more than to run a* hotel *like a servant*, he had sneered at his father, when he'd imagined such words could hurt Spyros's feelings, back when he was young and assumed his father had any—he intended to win a decisive battle in this war with his wife.

Once and for all.

CHAPTER FIVE

O<small>N THE OFF</small> chance that he had merely said that *man and wife* nonsense for the pleasure of alarming her—and how she hated to admit he'd succeeded—Jolie took the fifteen or so minutes she had left before evening drinks usually began to go and see for herself.

Surely even Apostolis would not be *that* peremptory.

But he'd been telling the truth. The back house where she'd lived and worked for seven years now looked like…any other part of the hotel. Quietly welcoming and richly appointed to best suit the island and the Andromeda's reputation for elegance, but stripped of anything personal.

Her heart hit against her ribs so hard it was a wonder a bone didn't crack from the impact.

With a sense of mounting horror—because surely that was what all the warring sensations inside her were, that weight in her belly and a tingle that was much too close to a kind of shiver radiating out from it—she left the back house and went over to the carriage house instead, walking in briskly the way she always did.

She had always thought of this house as a temple

to all the things that were wrong with his family, and Apostolis specifically. There was the office that she now shared with Apostolis, that Apostolis had claimed with a huge, black desk years ago. It took up the lion's share of the space in the office and was a particularly odd choice for a man who…had not worked here until his father had passed.

Then again, he seemed to think she was only there to play on the internet, as if she didn't have a mobile.

Though she would have died before commenting on it.

But the house announced itself in the entry hall. It started with the row of black-and-white photographs that lined the walls, framed to better proclaim their self-importance, as each and every one had been taken by a world-famous photographer who had been a guest here. Spyros had liked to say that he'd traded the bill for their stays for the photographs, but Jolie didn't have to be familiar with the hotel's books to know that was untrue.

Spyros loved a good story, but he loved money more.

Her heart was performing cartwheels inside her chest now that she'd made her way inside. She told herself—rather sternly—not to react to the place as if it, too, was waging a battle against her.

"It's just a house," she told herself crossly.

That was true. It was a house. That worked well enough when she was here to deal with hotel business. But it was *his* house. And tonight she was here because he'd moved *her* into this house.

With him.

Instead of heading down the hall to the office, she turned the other direction instead, and hated it.

The ground floor was lovely, having long ago been opened up to let in the light, and was now a flowing, open space that included a kitchen, a dining area, and a living room with doors that led out to the carriage house's private patio. She walked through all the white and blue and vivid accents, aware of the sea watching her from outside the windows and the excruciatingly modern art on the walls that always seemed to sit in judgment of her.

"Three splashes of paint on a canvas cannot *judge* anyone," she muttered as she passed a particularly snobbish painting on her way to the open, winding stair that rose up from the ground floor to the open gallery that ran above it.

Jolie ran up the steps, her feet tapping out a staccato that was still too slow to match her pulse. Upstairs, there were low-slung leather couches and views of the ocean, and sculpture pieces in recessed alcoves.

But she was here to check the bedrooms for her things, so that was what she did. Jolie's heart was still clattering about, but she was starting to feel almost... giggly. That was new and shocking enough to make her stop short.

Then she remembered the sort of silly games she and the other girls had got up to at school, sneaking about the place after curfew for the sheer joy of...not being where they were supposed to be.

It felt like breaking the rules to be up on this floor,

and it must have always felt that way, because she'd never come up here before.

"Focus," she ordered herself, marching down the hall that led off the gallery and opening up doors as she went.

One room was clearly a guest room, and given Apostolis's lack of guests, Jolie doubted it had been used in years. The next room looked as if it could be converted into guest quarters if necessary, though it was currently doing duty as another sort of library, with books stacked neatly on every surface, which made her feel...odd.

Was Apostolis a reader? Or was this overflow from the Andromeda's library? She didn't know which answer she wanted more. She didn't know which one would make her feel better. Or worse.

Maybe she didn't know how she wanted to feel about any of this.

Take Dioni, who had gotten strange over the past few weeks. Jolie had wondered if it was a reaction to her friend marrying her brother. If Dioni hadn't minded when Jolie was married to her *father*, but Apostolis, who Dioni had always looked up to, was something else no matter that she'd initially celebrated it. Because Dioni hadn't felt that Jolie marrying Spyros was really anything but a bit of a personal tragedy for her friend, but great news for *her,* because she got to have her best friend around all the time.

But Dioni was not a liar, and she had nothing but positive things to say about Jolie's marriage.

Maybe, she had whispered fiercely on the tarmac, *my brother and you will find what you need in each other.*

And she had sounded so hopeful. Jolie hadn't had the heart to tell her that Apostolis had never been even remotely heroic—not to Jolie.

That was something he saved for his sister.

In the car ride back, she'd had to face the fact that Dioni, for the first time in as long as Jolie had known her, was keeping secrets. Like why she suddenly wanted to move halfway across the planet, alone, when she'd never indicated the slightest interest in such adventurousness before.

She should have been proud. She had always told her friend that she needed to go out there and *claim her life*.

Jolie should have specified that she hadn't meant that Dioni should do that while leaving *her* behind, neck-deep in another round of her *choices*.

She was going to miss her best friend terribly.

She already did.

It made her tell the blasted man things she shouldn't. He made her forget herself, and that was unforgivable.

She blew out a breath, there in the hall. Calm was what was needed, not more storming about lighting fires. After all, she'd already done seven years in this lovely prison. What were five more? There was no need for more fire, thank you.

Jolie chanted that to herself as she opened the larger door at the end of the hall and all her breath deserted her in a rush.

Because this was clearly the master bedroom. *His* bedroom.

She drifted in, feeling jumpy. As if she expected to trip an alarm, when that was silly. She knew where all the security measures were in this house and all the other buildings on hotel property.

But her gaze was drawn immediately to the bedside tables, where some member of staff had carefully stacked the things she'd had on a similar table in her room in the other house. Just so.

It made tears prick at the backs of her eyes, and a lump fill her throat.

It was *not good,* she told herself.

She whirled around, seeing a succession of spaces that were clearly meant to mimic the flow below. But she found her way into a massive dressing room, where she saw all of her clothes. Just *hanging* there, suggesting an intimacy with all of *his* clothes.

As if their clothes were more married than they were.

Jolie had to put her hand out to the nearest wall to steady herself. From the surge of *fury* that swept over her. Because this was clearly a moment of *temper,* she assured herself, as her body…*reacted.*

And then kept reacting.

She dashed a hand over her eyes. Did he truly believe that he could simply…move her things in and that would be that? That he could simply *decide* that it was time to commence a relationship that involved *sharing a bed* when they'd never agreed to anything of the kind?

When they'd never discussed it at all?

Jolie refused.

And she was certain that that rushing sensation in her body and the way it all pulled down low into her belly—almost uncomfortably hot, like *fury* or *flu*—was confirmation that he was out of his mind.

But she made herself take a long, steadying breath. She pushed away from the wall and went into the attached bathroom suite, so she could check her face and make sure she looked nothing but effortless.

Because he wasn't the only one who could play mind games.

After a quick stop at the hotel's front desk, she drifted out onto the terrace where the family that had been staying with them for weeks now was already gathered. The adults were enjoying their drinks and talking in low, happy voices as they looked out at the sea far below, waiting for another one of the predictably spectacular Mediterranean sunsets.

She found Apostolis at once, and all of that chaos and riot inside of her seem to spiral into a kind of sharp focus.

So sharp it almost hurt.

Jolie smiled, murmuring greetings to the guests as she passed, and then went directly to her husband to slip her arm through his and even hug it a little, as if they were close like that. She knew exactly how to make it seem as if they possessed a deeply physical connection, and so she did that, too. All it took was tilting her head up to look at him and smiling a bit dreamily as he looked down at her, his dark gaze burning hot.

And deeply wary.

Good, she thought.

"I'm so sorry I'm late," she said in a voice calculated to *accidentally* reach everyone. Then she offered the guests a faintly sheepish smile, as if surprised they'd heard her. "My only excuse is that I am a newlywed again. I never expected such a thing to happen."

It was like she'd changed the temperature with a flip of a switch, because suddenly everyone was all smiles. And open in a way they hadn't been, not quite, since they'd arrived. There had been too much speculation, too many whispers, too many raised brows.

But this new spirit of openness went on all evening.

Perhaps because of this, the family invited their hosts to have dinner with them. They all sat around the great table beneath the pergola, basking in the soft evening breeze, with its hint of salt and flowers in the air.

"We did wonder," said the matriarch, sitting next to Jolie and even pressing her shoulder against hers. "There has been a great deal of talk about the changes here, as I'm sure you can imagine."

"It's been a time of transition," Jolie said with a nod. "It's hard not to talk about that, I suppose, when it involves a place that means so much to all of us."

"Spyros was a dear old man who everyone knows you loved well," said the older woman, and Jolie knew that her *everyone* encompassed more people than simply the family members she gathered here each year to celebrate her birthday. "We all thought so. But you are a young woman with her whole life ahead of her. And what is it they say? *The heart wants what it wants.*" She smiled then, as if dispensing her good favor. "I think that a brand-new love story is exactly what the Andromeda needs."

Jolie reached over and put her hand on the old woman's hand. "I can't tell you what it means to me that you understand," she told her softly. "I know how it must look from the outside, but..."

She trailed off helplessly, and it was true that she meant to do that. To sound so helpless in the face of the *Apostolis* of it all. But it was also true that her heart had not calmed down at all. And she was beginning to suspect that neither fury nor flu had anything to do with the situation inside of her.

A situation that was not getting better the longer she sat here, playing a woman *madly and recklessly in love.*

"Anyone who looks at the two of you can see the chemistry between you," said her guest, with a bit too much confidence for Jolie's peace of mind—but she reminded herself that she wanted that. That it was a commentary on the act she was putting on and no more. No one knew what was happening inside of her. No one—including herself, if she was honest. "Just as anyone who saw you and Spyros could tell that what you had was real, not what they liked to hint in the papers. Don't you worry, child. Real love *always* wins over the gossips."

Jolie murmured her thanks. And when she lifted her hand from the woman's and shifted her gaze across the table, Apostolis was gazing straight at her.

Very much as if *he* knew exactly what was happening inside her. All of that heat and weight and helpless wonder, God help her.

She found it *hurt* to tug her gaze away from his.

It was a long evening, filled with wine, conversation, laughter, and reminiscing. Sometimes she lost herself in moments like these and pretended she really was the mysterious and yet approachable hostess they thought she was, elegant and endearing in turn. Sometimes she forgot that these were roles that she played, not versions of her *actual self*. If she squinted, she could almost imagine that what the canny old woman had said about her was true. That she and Spyros had really had that kind of affection between them. Or that she and Apostolis had fallen head over heels in love.

That she'd really fallen into that kind of charmed life, here in one of the most beautiful places on earth.

And because there was an audience, because there was always an audience, she made sure that was exactly what it looked like.

At the end of the evening, when everything had been cleared away, she and Apostolis waved good-night to the guests. Then they walked back across the drive and she took the act one step further, threading her fingers through his and she turned back to wave over her shoulder once more.

His fingers closed over hers, tight. As if he had no intention of letting her go. And she could feel the tension in him. That humming awareness that she knew was in her, too, though she doubted it was for the same reason.

Hers involved the side of righteousness, after all.

She let herself droop almost languidly into him as they crossed the drive, enjoying the way he tensed the whole of his big, hard body at the contact. Then they went into the carriage house like they were exiting a stage.

Jolie went first. Apostolis followed. It was a perfect rendition of *careful*.

But once inside, she turned to him and laughed.

Right there in the hall, in front of all the artsy photographs of happy moments that she doubted had ever been as happy as they seemed, she made sure that her laugh was almost too brittle to bear.

"What do you think of that performance?" she asked him, in a completely different voice than the soft, cultured, dreamy one she'd been using all night. "Did you like it? Do you think that I'll win an award now that the curtain's gone down?"

And it felt like a blast of sheer triumph when all he could do was stare at her. Jolie took a deep breath that felt as if it was shuddering all the way through her, but she told herself that was just another part of this victory. That Apostolis actually looked stunned.

So stunned that he couldn't even mask his reaction.

She laughed again. "Did you really think that you could just…move me into your bed? Without discussion? What planet do you live on?"

"I live on the planet where when I kiss you we both go up in flames," he shot back. Clearly no longer quite so stunned. And his eyes were on fire. "And unlike you, I'm not afraid to play in that fire. Can you say the same?"

She shook her head slowly, feeling a great wash of rage move over her. What else could it be, so hot and flushed and *furious?*

"I'm not afraid of anything involving you," she told

him, very deliberately. "My worst nightmare involving you has already come true."

"Prove it," he invited her, something more than a simple flame in his gaze.

"I don't have to prove it. All I have to do is pretend I'm sleeping with you and it achieves everything I need it to do. Why would I actually *do* it? What's in it for me?"

"I think you know that it's the last battlefield, Jolie."

"And I suppose you think that you have all the weapons necessary for victory?" She made a new opera out of the roll of her eyes, and the bored shake of her head. "How naïve you are. You forget, I think, that this is a marriage, not one of your tawdry affairs. We have no choice but to stay together for forty-four weeks of each and every one of the next five years. If you blow something up you might have to live in the rubble, Apostolis. You and I both know that you're not built to handle that."

It was his turn to laugh at something that wasn't funny at all. "You speak with great authority for a person who doesn't know anything of importance about me."

Jolie lifted a languid shoulder and tracked the way his gaze followed the movement. "The only thing I need to know about you is that you've never stuck anything out. On the other hand, I was married to your father for years. And contrary to what our guests seem to think, it was not exactly a trip through the tulips. It was work." But she didn't want to get into that, so she kept going, especially when she saw the query in his gaze. "What do you know about that kind of work? I mean real work. The gritty intimacy involved in having not only to live with the decisions you make, but to marinate in the consequences of those decisions day after day, year after year."

"Has it happened?" he asked, she realized somewhat dimly that he had moved closer, then, because her back was suddenly against the wall. And the only thing she could see was him. "Have we finally arrived at the moment where you admit that your reasons for marrying my father were mercenary, that he was a monster, and that you were miserable?"

"I envy you," Jolie told him softly. "What a gift it is that you could reach your advanced age and still believe things could be so black and white. I'm afraid that privilege was taken from me quite early. And I have nothing to complain about in my life. I have been well provided for, with only a short period of anxiety about such things. On the other end of the next five years, I will be able to do as I please. I'm not sure that I would change any of it if I could."

Jolie had never said that out loud before. She wasn't sure she had even thought it. Because that was the trouble with regret, wasn't it? With peering back through time, imagining that the things that haunted her could be taken away somehow... If they were, then it meant everything else would also change. She could have ignored Spyros when he'd turned his eye toward her, but where would she be now if she had?

She didn't have to imagine what Mathilde's fate

would have been if she'd turned him down. The possibilities were etched on the inside of her eyelids.

"You're such a liar," Apostolis said then, in a voice that was nearly crooning. Nearly soft, like a lover's. "Everything about you is a lie. What I can't decide is if you believe the lies you tell or if you are entirely callous, spitting them out one after the next like every other falsehearted grifter who ever lived."

That might have hurt, coming from someone else. And she felt a phantom pain in the vicinity of her chest anyway. She told herself she was imagining what that would feel like if he'd mattered to her at all.

"That sounds a lot like projecting," she said, lightly. Easily. As if she had never been hurt by a thing in all her days here, and certainly not by *him*. "Once again, I think you'd be an excellent candidate for therapy. And no need to worry. It would only take... Oh, I don't know. Twenty years or so to untangle all these things in you that have become so rotted and terrible." She reached out and patted him on the arm, her smile fairly dripping with false sweetness. "Trust the process, Apostolis. You can do it."

He laughed again, then, and there was something about it. The way it rolled through her, and him, too. She could see it. Or she could feel it, maybe, something shimmering and starkly dangerous, winding around the pair of them and filling up the hall.

Filling up the whole house.

That was when Jolie realized that, possibly for the first time, they were truly all alone.

Not in a moving vehicle. Not in a place where staff

might appear at any moment, because they never came here without an invitation and an appointment.

Dioni was flying across the Atlantic even now.

That meant it was just the two of them and this wild, chaotic war of theirs. She could hear the beat of those war drums, a deep *insistence* within her. She could feel the march of booted feet, up and down her spine.

"There are only so many ways this can end." And there was still that dangerous laughter all over his face. It made his eyes gleam in that way they did sometimes, that bittersweet gold. "We could kill each other. For obvious reasons, I would prefer to avoid that. One of us could kill the other. For legal reasons, I can't support that either. But if we continue like this, constantly upping the ante, constantly trying to outwit the other, it's going to be one of those two endings. I hope you know that."

"Spoken as someone who, once again, can only imagine things in the short term." Jolie leaned back against the wall and crossed her arms. Then tilted up her chin, hoping she looked as insouciant as she wished she felt. "And more than that, only thinks with one part of his anatomy. None of this is a surprise to me, you understand. But I think you're going to have to learn that not everything can be solved in the way you think it ought to be, just because *you* lack imagination."

"What amazes me is that you think that headlines are facts, Jolie, when I would think you'd know better, personally. And I suppose it would be easier for you if I really did only think with one part of my anatomy. But your tragedy is that, deep down, you know I'm right."

He moved forward then, just a little. Just enough to make her brace herself—

But she shouldn't have.

Because doing so gave away too much. She knew it instantly.

His smile confirmed it. "You might have had my father wrapped around your finger. You might have been the one who used sex as a weapon in that relationship. But in this one?"

This time he leaned even closer, bracing himself with one palm on the wall beside her head. She thought for a terrible, thrilling moment that he might actually put his mouth on hers once more—

But he didn't. He put his mouth to her ear instead.

"This time the best you can hope for is mutually assured destruction," he whispered, and she suspected he knew the way the sound and *feel* of those words curled through her like smoke and warning. "And I have to tell you, my darling stepmother and wife, I think that *my* destruction is highly unlikely."

Words crowded into her mouth as if fighting to get out, but Jolie did not allow herself a retort. She angled herself back, only slightly. Partly because the wall was at her back, but more importantly, because he was *right there*, still bracing himself against the wall.

Still leaning over her.

She found his gaze, bittersweet and gleaming, and held it.

Then, so slowly it was almost like *thinking* about moving instead of moving, she reached out. She trailed her fingers over his face, noting that when he took a swift and surprised breath, it was as if she could feel it inside her, too.

And that wasn't all she could feel. Touching him felt remarkably like touching herself. She could feel the trail of sensation. She could feel the way it moved in her, a slow, languorous heat.

Jolie moved her hand from his face to touch the side of his neck, and his collarbone, sneaking her fingers beneath the open collar of his shirt to test the rich warmth of his skin. There was a hint of the hair that she already knew dusted his chest and went all the way down to below his navel. A thing she wished she hadn't known, if she was honest. But she had seen him once, years before, coming out of the sea with water cascading all over his toned body and making him gleam in the Greek sun.

Gleam even more than he usually did, that was.

In this moment, she could admit that she had held that image close all this time. But then, she felt about images of him the same way she felt about sugar. Of course she liked the taste of it. Who wouldn't?

Maybe it was time she admitted that *hatred* was the thing she hid behind when it came to this man, because there was *this* underneath.

Maybe it had been there all along.

She had never felt anything like it before, and she had been marrying his father when she'd met him, so how could she have called it what it was?

But acknowledging that uncomfortable truth didn't change anything. If she allowed herself to indulge, just like sugar, she paid for it for too long after to make the indulgence worthwhile.

Down and down she went, moving her hand outside of his shirt again so she could lazily trace the line of the buttons that held it together, all the way down to that hard-ridged abdomen that she'd just been remembering.

And then, her eyes still fixed to his, she moved lower still, and traced a pattern over that hard, proud ridge that already pushed against his trousers.

It grew even more when she settled her hand against it. He was hard. So very, very hard. And she could feel that hardness seemed to rebound through her, as if he was already deep inside of her body.

Jolie had never wanted him more than she did in this moment—but she wanted to win this battle more.

She angled herself closer, tipping her head up as if asking for a kiss. And she drank in the way his eyes went dark and greedy.

"Look at you," she whispered, huskily, pressing her hand against the length of him. "You look a little bit... destroyed, Apostolis. There are worse things than death after all, are there not? Like losing."

And then she ducked under his arm and headed for the stairs, moving across the flow of rooms and up the circular steps before she even dared look over her shoulder. Her heart was pounding too hard for her to hear anything. The heat of the hardest part of him was a brand across her palm.

And she was not sure if he was right there on her heels, or still down below.

But when she looked, he stood at the bottom of the

stairs. He looked up at her, a tortured expression she had never seen before on his face. And she couldn't enjoy it the way she should have, because she worried she wore the same expression herself.

More, his chest was moving as if he'd run a marathon to get from the wall to the first stair.

And she felt that, too, like a touch.

"If I were you," he told her, his voice a dark ribbon through the dark of the house, with only the stars outside to bear witness to this, "I would run. While you can."

To her shame, there was a part of her that wanted to do just that, and run—but straight to him, so she could see where this fire went. So she could see if they would truly turn each other to ash after all—

But that was too close to surrender.

So she ran to the room that she'd chosen for herself, the guest room she'd made sure the staff had come and arranged for her while she'd been playing hostess games—taking all of her things out of *his* bedroom as if she'd never been there in the first place—and locked the door behind her.

Though as she lay there on the bed she'd made, wide awake and staring at the ceiling for far too long, she had to ask herself—had she really been locking *him* out?

Or herself in?

CHAPTER SIX

THE WAR WAS now begun in earnest, making it clear only minor skirmishes had happened before. All antes were upped. Survival was the only goal, and it was no foregone conclusion.

Apostolis had never felt so alive.

He told himself it was the thrill of his impending victory coming in hot, whether *she* thought that he would win or not.

He knew that he would.

Or in any case, that was what he told himself as the season rolled on. As one set of guests left and another arrived. As he was involved with handling the daily issues that cropped up at the hotel that he had only observed before from the distance his father insisted upon.

And was forced to face an unpalatable truth.

Jolie was not simply a trophy, as he'd thought. Or perhaps as he'd hoped.

She was an integral part of the hotel's operation.

In all the ways that mattered, she *was* the proprietor, and given the way the staff deferred to her in all things, clearly had been.

Perhaps since her marriage to his father.

It was entirely possible that was one of the reasons Spyros had married her, when he had never bothered to marry the other women he'd taken as lovers over the years.

He was forced to view the woman—his stepmother, his wife, his co-proprietor—in an entirely new light and he found himself longing for the dark.

Because the fact that Jolie was both good at the guest-facing parts of her job—the consummate hostess, a study in effortless and yet engaging mystery—as well as all the things that happened behind the scenes... annoyed him. It would have been easier if she'd been a disaster, or as useless as he'd expected—but then, if she had been, the hotel would have been in dire straits and that wouldn't have been any kind of victory.

Apostolis found himself torn between wanting to do nothing but come to a kind of reckoning with Jolie—and trying to understand his own relationship to the hotel that had stood as a cornerstone of his family for so long.

He talked often with Alceu, for a variety of reasons but also because his friend lived in what was more or less a fortress—though it was more delicately termed a *castle*—on the island of Sicily.

"You know what it is to care for a house that is more than a house, and that is considered more important than the family that lives in it," he said one day.

"It is called a legacy," Alceu replied in his usual arid tones. "A word I believe you are familiar with. And legacies require care and maintenance. Sometimes this is inconvenient. Very seldomly does it involve the attentions of supermodels or paparazzi, which I know is a significant lifestyle change for you."

"Thank you," Apostolis replied, perhaps more stiffly than he might have wished. "I am aware."

What he *wanted* to say was something like *Et tu, Brute?*

Though he knew that wasn't fair. Alceu had always been the more serious of the two of them. Or, perhaps, what he really meant was that Alceu had always known that his legacy was secured—and more, that said legacy would be his to steward.

He had not had to perform for his father's attention the way Apostolis had.

It was something Apostolis found seemed to weigh on him more and more, especially when his relationship with the co-owner of his hotel was fraught with all the other battles they were waging.

He found her in the office one morning, going through paperwork that he was certain he'd mentioned he had intended to get to himself.

Once he accepted that until now, she had been doing it in front of him and he had willfully ignored the possibility that she was actually…working.

It filled him with something he knew too well was not temper. Temper was easy. This lingered in his gut. It was too thick.

"Do you do this deliberately?" he asked her as he took in what she was working on, there in the large office suite in its own wing of the carriage house. "Do you ignore what you are told because it makes you feel better to think you're doing this all by yourself?"

"This might come as a great shock to you," Jolie replied to him in that sharply serene manner of hers, complete with that smile that might as well have been a dagger, "but I do not spend a great deal of time thinking about you at all."

He stopped at the desk where she was sitting, and leaned back against it so she had no choice but to lift her gaze to him. "Liar."

Jolie sat back in her chair, and he thought that while she might have looked languid from a distance—he was closer than that. That meant he could see the awareness in her gaze. He could see the faint hint of color in her cheeks.

No matter what she said, she was not unaffected.

And that, in turn, affected him.

Tremendously.

But he knew better than to show his hand again so soon. That night when she'd teased him and left him standing there in the hall, wild with frustrated need, haunted him.

In more ways than one.

Back when he'd believed she was a useless bit of fluff he could simply maneuver around as he pleased.

"What is it that you want from this interaction, Apostolis?" she asked, and there was a hint of impatience in her voice—perhaps more than a hint—but he could see the truth in her gaze. There was a heat there that had nothing to do with *impatience*. He could read that, clear as day. "I walked into the office this morning, these things weren't done, and so I'm doing them. That's all it is. Not everything is a plot against you." She shook her head as if she'd never heard of something so silly. "Why do you think that it is?"

Apostolis thought about the conversation that he'd had with Alceu. And he also thought about strategy. He told himself it had nothing to do with the fact that she wasn't looking at him as if he was a science experiment when she asked the question.

Not at the moment, anyway. She looked as if she was genuinely interested.

"Have you not heard?" he asked lightly. "My father was always disappointed in my business acumen. I feel certain he would have mentioned it. He and I spoke of very little else on the rare occasions we spoke."

"Your father liked cocktail parties," she replied in the same tone. "He left the business to me. And that was a fairly overwhelming task, most days, so I did not spend a lot of time worrying about anyone else's *business acumen*."

He frowned at that. "What are you saying? He can't possibly have let you run the whole of the hotel business all on your—"

But he cut himself off, because why was he astonished to hear such a thing? He was well-versed in his father's hypocrisy. He had lived it.

"Your father had a business manager many years ago to do all of this. Firing him was one of the first things I did when I arrived." Her smile sharpened as she looked up at him, as if defying him to argue once again that none of this could be true. That he still doubted what he had seen unfold in all parts of the hotel, before his very eyes, since their marriage. "And if you're wondering if anyone took a young woman like me seriously at first, the answer is no. Of course they didn't. But it didn't matter. Your father wanted to continue on as he had always done. He liked to be the life of the party, but he didn't like to *plan* the party. And as it turns out, my education made me a perfect fit for party planner extraordinaire."

They both seemed to realize they were actually *talking* to each other for a change at the same time. It clearly shook her as much as it did him.

Jolie stood. Apostolis straightened from the desk.

For a moment, maybe two, they frowned at each other as if there was a *trick*, here. As if one of them had *done something* to force this unheard-of moment of accord.

"And here I thought your marriage to my father was blissful in every regard," he heard himself say, but it wasn't as scathing as he'd meant it to be.

Surely he'd *meant* it to be.

"It had its ups and downs." Jolie's chin rose just slightly as she said it. Just enough to hint at defiance without entirely committing to it. "You seem overly interested in my previous relationship. If I were you, I'd worry a little bit more about this one."

"But I have heard your relationship with my father described as *affectionate,*" he reminded her, with, perhaps a little too much sardonic inflection in his voice, if such a thing existed. "Surely this cannot all have been a mirage."

Her eyes flashed and he expected her to strike back at him—but instead, she shook her head. A bit as if she despaired of him. Or was exhausted by him.

Not the reaction most women had to his presence, he could admit.

"You think that everything is about greed," she said in her quiet way that still managed to land hard. "That tells me that the only thing you think about is greediness—maybe other people's, maybe your own. Meanwhile, there are other reasons in this world to do things that others might find unpalatable. That you might find hard to bear yourself. I'm happy for you, Apostolis, that you've never had to make such choices."

This was as close to an admission that things had not been wonderful with his father as she'd ever given him.

"Tell me," he said, suddenly seized with an urgency that he did not understand. "Just once, tell me the truth. Why did you marry him?"

Something exquisitely sad moved over Jolie's face at that, and as if she knew it, or sensed it, she looked away. Out the window toward another bright and sunny Mediterranean day unfolding spectacularly before them. The sunlight outside fell on her face and he was struck once more by the fact that this woman was truly flawless.

That even bright, direct light did not *reveal* her. It only enhanced her beauty.

"I made a practical decision," she told him, as if this topic made her tired. "And I would make the same decision again." She looked back at him then, but the expression on her face had changed. It was more opaque now. There was no trace of any *sadness*. "I had no idea you were such a romantic, Apostolis. I confess, I'm shocked."

"The chasm between mercenary and romantic is almost as vast and wide as your capacity for lying," he said, but almost…conversationally. As if they were having a friendly chat. *Almost*. "What I wonder is if you're lying to yourself as well as everyone else."

Her eyes narrowed slightly, but that was the only reaction she saw on her face. Her lovely, flawless face, like a work of art.

"Mercenary is such an interesting word," she murmured.

She crossed her arms in that neat way she had that made it look like an elegant way to hold them, not a gesture stemming from any kind of anger or negative feeling. Everything with her was that kind of performance, he knew. Everything about her was calculated.

He wasn't sure what the matter was with him that he should find that something to admire.

"Is it really all that interesting?" he asked. "Or does it describe a set of behaviors—for the sake of argument, let's say *your* behaviors—perfectly?"

She let her mouth curve into something gracious. She did not unfold her arms. "For the sake of argument, let us take the son of a very wealthy man. A case study, if you will. A son who had the very best of everything, always. An upbringing of well-documented ease, waited upon hand and foot by servants, and then sent off to some of the finest schools in the world."

She lifted a hand and he realized that he was frowning. Possibly even scowling. "This is not to say that there were not stumbling blocks," she allowed. "Or periods of grief and disappointment. It is a life, after all. But let's say that time goes on for our wealthy man's son. Some people would be forced to find employment. Others might decide that they need employment. Not for money, in the case of our heir to everything, but because every person needs some form of industry to feel fulfilled as a human." She shook her head, almost fondly. "But not our golden son. He prefers instead to live off the proceeds of his various trust funds. He wafts about, making a case for gluttony and self-indulgence, year after year after year. Because, of course, there is no point in him chaining himself to some other profession when his true profession awaits. Like any little princeling, his entire life involves marking time, waiting for his father to die. Only then can he assume control of the whole family fortune, not merely his little sliver of it. Only then can he truly *do something* with his life, such as it is, and assuming he knows how to go about it after all that laziness."

Again, that curve of her lips. "But you have the audacity to call *me* mercenary."

The urge to simply strike back at her was so intense that Apostolis was shocked it didn't take him from his feet.

Instead, he thought of her hand, tracing its way down the length of his torso. He thought of the way she had gripped his sex, just enough to make him imagine the kind of things that they could do to each other—and in more detail than he already had by that point.

He had thought of little else since.

And it was growing harder and harder to convince himself that these thoughts had a basis in anything but the most intense desire he had ever known.

Then again, Apostolis acknowledged that sometimes, choosing the less obvious weapon was the better strategic choice. It couldn't all be rocket launchers and carpet bombs.

"I shouldn't be surprised that you are so imaginative," he drawled, choosing not to focus on *desire*. "It almost hurts me to tell you that I'm afraid you've got it all wrong. I've never touched any of the money held in trust for me. And not, I can admit, by my own choice. Not at first."

He was questioning the wisdom of this line of conversation, so he turned away from her, going over to look out of the window himself. The Andromeda rose, stately and reserved, as if some kind of counterweight to all of that impossible Mediterranean sunshine that streamed all around it so recklessly.

While in the distance, always, glinted the deep blue of the sea.

And as always, these things soothed him. No matter how many ghosts there might have been hanging about. No matter how many memories and regrets seemed to sink into his skin, simply by his being here again.

"Old Spyros felt that my attitude was lacking," he said, staring out at the sea but seeing only those ghosts and regrets. Those memories he'd never been able to shake. "Or perhaps, that week, he didn't like my tone. It's so hard to remember. But at some point, not long after I left university, he decided that cutting me off would be the making of me."

He looked back over his shoulder to find her watching him, and decided that it would do him no good to attempt to categorize the expression she wore her face just then. It would haunt him enough as it was, with that ferocious way she was listening to him. As if it took the whole of her body.

"The irony, you understand, is that Spyros himself never worked a day in his life," he continued. "He was committed to behaving atrociously right up until my grandfather died. Entirely to be done with him, some claim. But by the time I had the temerity to enjoy myself, too, he fancied himself quite the man of business. No son of *his,* etcetera. So there I was. The princeling you imagine, but tragically with no access to the funds that could keep me in the lifestyle I preferred."

"He cut you off?" She was frowning now herself. "That's not the way he told it."

"As such a fan of great fictions yourself, I would have thought you would understand by now that there were few more dedicated storytellers than my father. Particularly when it came to his own behavior." He turned to face her fully then, leaning back against the windowsill and watching the sunlight dance all over her, lighting her up. "I could have come back here and spent the past years loafing about the islands, making myself disreputable beyond any reasonable doubt. Instead, my friend Alceu, no stranger to familial disputes himself, suggested that rather than waste our twenties in the manner of so many of our peers, we might go about making our own money. So that whatever happened in the future, we would never have to depend on handouts ever again."

He was shocking her, and he liked it, though it did make him wonder what exactly his father had told her.

Not because he cared what Spyros had said about anything. That realization surprised him, because it came with another, even more shocking one. It was because he cared what *she* thought.

That this was a clear indication that he was, perhaps, not as in control of this particular skirmish as he might wish was obvious. But there was no stopping now. "Alceu is formidable. Always. I am...charming. Together, we make a rather devastating team. No one ever sees us coming."

"What is it you do?" she asked.

And something shifted inside of him, down deep. Because he'd expected her to laugh at the idea, he realized, the way his father had when he'd even hinted that he and Alceu were handling themselves, thank you.

But it was more than that. He would have sworn on any stack of holy books offered to him that this was the very first time Jolie had ever asked him a completely honest question, without any edge to it.

He wanted to savor it. Instead, he shrugged. "We buy things," he told her. "And we saw that sometimes the things we bought required...refurbishment. So we took it upon ourselves to provide it. When we're done, we sell them on."

That was more or less true.

"Are you talking about…antiques? Or something more like a corporation?"

"Alceu is particularly well attuned to locating the wounded," Apostolis said after a moment's consideration. "It is as if he can sniff them out. Whether it is an estate, a hotel, a corporation, it doesn't matter. If it has a weakness, Alceu will know it. Often before the entity in question does. In the beginning, we were concerned with selling ourselves to these entities, to prove what we could do. Now we simply offer something too good to be refused."

Her blue eyes glinted. "And this is what you do. You swan about bullying people and making money off of misery."

"Never that," he said, instantly. "We fix broken things, Jolie. We paste them back together and make them better than new. And when we leave, we leave the things we've fixed happier than when we found them." He laughed when he saw her skeptical expression. "You do not have to believe me. I cannot say that I care if you do or not."

That was…not as true as he wanted it to be, so he pushed on. "But I can tell you that Alceu informed me some years ago that if he did not know me personally, he would have put the Andromeda on our list." This was the sticky bit, and he was almost unwilling to do it. He reminded himself that this was a strategy, that was all. It was an admission that he had been forced to make to himself once he'd realized the truth. And then, today, the *extent* of that truth. "Before you, that is."

He heard her sharp, indrawn breath. He saw the way she stiffened. "I don't know what you mean."

"You do." He waved a hand over the desk where she'd been sitting. "My father cared only about the party, as you said. This is not under dispute. But seven years ago, there was suddenly a steady hand on the wheel. And now the hotel is no longer bleeding out its resources in every possible direction. I know exactly who is responsible for that."

"Your father gave me free rein with the office work," she said, though she looked guarded. "I assume that might be one of the reasons he left me part of the hotel. He clearly knew that you didn't need his money."

"But you did need the money," he said, softly. He had anticipated playing this particular card later, but something told him it was better to do it now. "Did he tell you to take a salary?"

"He insisted upon it."

"It is not very difficult to track money, if you know where to look," Apostolis said softly. Very softly, and he saw her spine straighten. That was what happened when secrets were exposed. "What I have noticed is that every time money goes into your account, you take ninety percent of it and send it back out again." He watched her closely. "Why?"

And for a moment, she looked…panicked.

It was the only word that fit, and he wasn't sure that he quite believed it. Jolie Girard Adrianakis…*panicked?* He couldn't imagine what that meant. It was certainly not the response of the hardened mercenary he'd expected. Or that of the Andromeda's proprietor and personal savior.

If he had been under the impression that she was somehow larcenous, which he hadn't been, he might have expected to see a hint of panic—but not like this. Apostolis had intended to simply note that there were no more secrets between them. That he knew every move she made.

And, yes, he had wanted very much to watch her reaction to that reality.

Now she looked as if he'd gone over and punched her in the stomach.

Looking *caught* was different from this, whatever *this* was.

He almost moved toward her, but held himself back—and it was harder to do than it should have been.

"What does it matter what I do with money I've earned?" she asked, but her usual fire was gone. If anything, she sounded shaky.

"You should consider trusting your husband," he replied.

"But I don't." And her chin tipped up, as if she was remembering herself in her defiance. "I don't trust my husband. I didn't trust my first husband and I trust my second husband even less."

"As someone who knew Spyros well, I find that difficult to believe."

"Spyros was always exactly who he said he was," Jolie told him with a laugh. Though it sounded strained. "For better or worse, what you saw was what you got. The same can't be said about you."

He did not give in to the urge to interrogate her on that—though he realized that she wanted him to. She *wanted* him to lose the thread of this conversation, so that they got back to talking about him instead of her.

"You do not send this money to the same place every time," he said, to make sure she knew he wasn't bluffing. That he really did know. "But you send it all the same, like clockwork." He considered her. "Who are you paying off? Who knows the truth about you, what is that truth, and why would you pay so much to keep it hidden?"

He could see that he taken a wrong turn, because her shoulders inched down from her ears. "Everyone deserves their own secrets, Apostolis. Even me."

He shook his head. "You do understand that I'm going to find out these answers on my own, I hope. And I'll tell you right now, Jolie, that it can only go better for you if I hear them from you first."

But he'd lost her. There was no hint of panic anywhere on her now. On the contrary, she looked almost lazy and amused, instead.

"Well then," she said, as patronizingly as possible, "I certainly hope I wrap up all of my nefarious doings before that occurs. Though what do you think will happen either way? We still have to be married to each other the next five years. Or have you forgotten?"

"I cannot imagine that I will ever forget," he shot back.

"Did you think the exchange of confidences would make *me* confide in *you?*" she asked, as if astonished. "You did, didn't you? You thought you would lead me, all unknowing, into some or other moment of vulnerability." She sighed at that. "Haven't you learned yet? I'm better at this game than you are."

"I'm glad you think so," he replied, and he was. "Because all that means to me is that you're not ready for what's coming. Given we both already know you're not clever enough to keep all your trespasses hidden."

And to his surprise, then, and something else—something like the light that was dancing all over her like it was specifically attracted to her—Jolie tossed back her head and laughed.

It wasn't a soft laugh. It was sharp and pointed and he was certain he could feel its talons, deep inside him.

"You've caught me," she said after a little too long with all that laughing. "I'm an idiot. Aren't you smart, Apostolis, to work that out so quickly."

She couldn't have been more sarcastic if she tried.

And maybe that was why he found himself closing the space between them.

The only thing he could think about was giving her back that laugh, with interest. All he could think about was restitution, especially when her blue eyes took on that challenging gleam that he'd last seen when her hand was on his sex—

And he didn't know what might have happened if the door to the office didn't open then.

If one of the staff members didn't stand there, looking apologetic. "I'm so sorry to interrupt," the woman said, looking back and forth between the two of them in a mix of alarm and speculation. "But the guests are asking for a host?"

"Allow me," murmured Jolie. It was only as she stepped around him that he realized how close to her that he had been standing. How much his hands actually twitched with the desire to get them on her, and all over her.

She glanced back at him when she reached the door as if she expected Apostolis might lunge after her. As if he was that far gone.

Then again...wasn't he?

Moving her into the carriage house had been a tactical error. He was certain that she disturbed the very air that he breathed, simply by existing in the same space. Sometimes he thought he could find traces of her scent...everywhere.

In rooms she wasn't in. When he woke in the night, his heart pounding thanks to one more distractingly detailed dream about the two of them wrapped together, rolling over and over each other in his bed.

Literally anywhere and everywhere, she made her presence known.

Maybe she could see these things stamped all over his face. Because once again, her lips curved and her blue eyes gleamed. And then she shut the door behind her.

Quietly, as if to indicate that *she* was unbothered by this *thing* between them.

But she left him with a puzzle to solve, above and beyond the maddening fact that he wanted this woman who seemed determined to keep him at a distance.

It wasn't that she didn't want him. He knew better than that. And that wasn't his ego talking, though he was fully aware that he possessed one of remarkable size.

He didn't have to put his hands on her to know a truth as stark as the one they'd both tasted when he'd kissed her. The same one he'd showed her the night she'd run her hand down his body.

Apostolis wasn't sure when he'd accepted that he was not only attracted to her, but that he always had been. It had been its own slow simmer. And it was difficult not to torture himself with wondering if she'd known exactly how he ached for her since the very beginning of her marriage to his father. If his father had known it. If it was that bleedingly obvious to everyone else alive.

But that didn't matter.

He crossed back over to the window and this time, he braced his hands on either side of the glass.

What mattered was that it was only a matter of time before he had her.

He understood that. And he couldn't know if Jolie had accepted that inevitability yet, but he had. There was a certain peace in that, because there was no need to push for something that was inevitable. There was no need to worry himself over something that was as unavoidable as day following night.

It was only a matter of time.

But that being so, finding out what secrets she was keeping became more important than ever.

He went over to his laptop, taking his chair at the obnoxiously huge desk that took over the room, a monument he'd placed here to annoy his father when he was not around to do it himself.

But he wasn't thinking about Spyros. He was determined that this time, he would know the answers to the questions he asked her before he asked them. The better to plan how and when to ask them at all.

Because there was no better way to break someone down than to peel them open.

And when it came to the frustrating enigma that was Jolie, his wife in almost no way but legally, he had to believe it was the most important weapon of all.

CHAPTER SEVEN

IT WAS LOWERING indeed to realize that if it weren't for Mathilde, she would have run.

Locked away in her little room some few evenings later—and still not sure if she was locking him out or herself in—Jolie found herself grappling with that deeply unflattering and unpalatable truth.

"Then again," she muttered aloud, glaring out her window toward the Andromeda, "if it weren't for Mathilde, I could have moved to any city in Europe and found myself some kind of job after I graduated."

Sometimes she dreamed about the life she might have had if she'd gone that route—but it was something she'd discussed at length with the headmistress over the course of her last year at the school. She'd gone around and around about her prospects.

Until the day the older woman had looked at her, once again with entirely too much knowledge in her gaze.

Listen to me, she had said. *I believe that all women should be as independent as possible, but there is a fine line between independent-minded and foolish. Right now you are penniless.*

She had said that with the precision of a knife thrust in deep.

It would be different if you had something to fall back on while you looked for an appropriate situation somewhere, but you don't. The rest of these girls, with their trusts and their funds and their wealthy families...

She had shaken her head, her gaze kind—but certain.

They have more options than you do, I am afraid. It's not that I think you can't find a decent life for yourself, Jolie. I just worry that you don't have enough time.

I'm hardly over the hill just yet, Jolie had protested.

I'm not talking about your prospects. The headmistress had shaken her head. *I'm talking about poverty. Everyone thinks that there is a huge gap between the rich and the poor, but the truth is that there is not as far to fall as most imagine. For most people, it's a very thin line. And the reality, my dear, is that you're already living on borrowed time. Your grandfather paid your tuition in full years ago, but you have nothing extra. You have no savings. How would you establish yourself somewhere in order to begin even looking for the kind of job you want? If you managed to secure a job, how would you afford a flat? Food? Transport?*

The headmistress had waved around at the castle-like building where she kept her office.

I worry that when you meet the real world, it will flatten you.

I've already survived—Jolie had started to argue.

But the headmistress had laid both her hands flat on the top of her desk. *I am not an heiress, Jolie. I grew up working-class. I had to scrape and worry over every bill, every day, when I was your age. And I had* significantly *more resources than you have right now. Do you understand what I'm telling you?*

The headmistress hadn't come out and said that she should think hard and fast about whether she wanted to find herself in the position of having to sell herself on a street corner to pay her rent. When she could instead make a bargain with a rich man who would keep her comfortable in most of the ways that mattered.

It was easy enough to tell which was the better option when it was offered to her.

And maybe the fact that she'd understood that there were worse things out there than a controlling old man and all his many demands had made it easier to inhabit her role as Spyros's scandalous younger wife. She had not found him *surprising.* He had not done a single thing she would call *unexpected* in the whole time she'd known him.

Except, she supposed, dying. She had expected him to live forever, if only to spite his son.

It was that son who was the problem.

It was Apostolis who had surprised her—floored her, completely, and not only because he wasn't the wastrel that she imagined. She had checked on that, of course. She certainly hadn't *taken his word for it.* But then, it hadn't taken much digging to find that everything he'd told her was true. She was forced to acknowledge that it had been Spyros who had asserted that Apostolis was a waste of space and she'd believed him, when the evidence was easily accessible all along.

And worse, he and his forbidding friend were not the soulless corporate raiders she'd imagined, but rather, *saviors*.

That was what the people they saved called them. That was how the companies and hotels and sometimes families they'd helped thought of them.

That had been upsetting enough.

But he also knew about the money she sent to her revolting aunt and uncle. Monthly.

Jolie couldn't risk that. She couldn't risk him knowing what she was doing because she was certain that if he did, he would somehow disrupt her payment plan— and then what would she do?

It had been made clear to her years before that even the slightest hiccup would be interpreted as a green light to go right ahead and use their daughter's greatest asset to enrich themselves as best they could.

And somehow, she very much doubted that her loathsome aunt and uncle would find a way to marry Mathilde off to a rich man the way Jolie had managed to do. She suspected it might be significantly more unsavory than that—possibly even those street corners that had haunted her all these years.

Even the thought of Mathilde at risk like that made her furious.

But she was running out of ways to control what was happening here. She knew that. She could feel the noose of all that awareness and fury between them tightening by the day.

"Too bad," she told herself sternly. "You don't get to mope about in your feelings."

Because it was already evening, and she had her duties to attend to, like it or not. She blew out a breath and got to her feet, then set about getting dressed for the night ahead. More drinks, more laughter. More confidences and effortless hostessing, whether she felt effortless or not.

And still more game playing, where her husband was concerned, which was…dangerous.

Because only Jolie knew, down deep in a place that she did not like to examine in the light of day, that sometimes, while she was playing this role for their guests, she pretended that it wasn't a role after all. She pretended that it was real, what she and Apostolis supposedly had together.

That they were lovestruck newlyweds, hardly able to bear *not* touching each other. All those lingering looks. Hands that found their way together and were difficult to part.

She pretended far too much, too often, and she very much feared that one of these days she was going to forget to disengage herself on the walk back to the carriage house. That she was going to forget to put her mask back into place when they were alone.

Worse still, there was a part of her that *wanted* that day to come. Even though she knew that was nothing short of madness.

Because every time she thought about surrendering to Apostolis Adrianakis in any regard, something deep inside of her sounded out a low, wild sort of tone. It seemed to reverberate all through her body, taking her over until all she could do was shake.

Deep inside where no one saw it, but she could feel it. ·Some days she felt nothing else.

And yet she knew that if she surrendered to him, she would never be the same.

Jolie padded down the circular stair, the shoes she wore barely a whisper over her feet so that she was entirely too aware of the *feel* of the steps beneath her feet. And as she walked through the open house toward the door, she was aware of everything else, too. The way the simple dress she'd decided to throw on seemed to caress her as she moved. The way the cool breeze from outside rushed in through the open glass doors to whisper its way over her skin. Even the necklace around her neck seemed to press against her the way his hand might flatten against the wall beside her head—

She rolled her eyes at her own fancy, something close enough to amused at her inability to keep her attention where it belonged. Or at least, away from the places where she knew better than to let it go.

Outside it was another magical Mediterranean evening. As she walked across the drive and the yard, it was so easy to let the beauty of this place wash away all the rest of it. It was so easy to pretend that these moments would be the bulk of the five years looming ahead of her, and not…the other moments. The more difficult ones.

She could hear the sounds of the guests before she rounded the corner of the hotel, and it felt natural for her lips to immediately curve into the specific shape she used for her public-facing duties. When she was doing her best to be enigmatic and alluring, the consummate hostess, beloved and yet a perfect, blank canvas for the guests to fill in as they pleased.

For a moment, right there at the corner of the building, she stopped. And she stood there, just beyond the terrace where she could see everyone there beneath the pergola wrapped in vines and twinkling lights, but no one could see her. Not unless they were looking for her specifically.

Their guests at present were a very famous singer and his expansive entourage of friends, backup singers, and longtime band members, some of whom stayed in the nearest village and went back and forth from there as they pleased. It meant that the terrace was filled with sparkling conversation, spontaneous bursts of music, and the sort of laid-back luxury that could only be achieved with a tremendous amount of money. Many of the faces she recognized, and not because she'd seen them here before. But because everyone had seen them, everywhere.

Yet her gaze skipped past all those famous visages and found him.

Apostolis, looking right back at her as if she was standing in a beaming spotlight instead of the shadows of the evening.

As if it was only the two of them out here tonight. As if the only thing between them was the sultry Greek air.

And even across the brightly clad, sophisticated group of cocktail partiers, Jolie could feel the weight of the way he looked at her. It was as if he trailed his fingers all over the surface of her skin from afar and she had no choice but to hum in reaction.

As if it was that or *combust* where she stood, eaten alive by all that sensation.

She felt certain he knew it, though there was only that faint curve in the corner of his mouth to make that clear. It occurred to her that she knew how to read him by now. And more, that the fact she could suggested a measure of intimacy with him that she wanted, badly, to deny.

But she couldn't.

And instead of walking onto the terrace to take up her duties, Jolie watched Apostolis instead—impressed despite herself that he was far better at this job than his father had ever been. At least during her tenure at the Andromeda.

She imagined the old man would turn over in his grave at the very thought. But that didn't make it any less true. Spyros had been overly impressed with his own legend. Toward the end of his life, he had believed that part of what the guests were paying for when they came here was *his* notoriety. *His* own considerable star power. The hotelier himself.

Apostolis did not sit as Spyros had done in his favorite corner of the terrace, holding court. He did not set himself apart from the guests, as if *he* was the guest of honor.

All the things that had made him such a tabloid staple, he put to good use here, with the guests. He made them laugh. He leaned closer as they poured out their confidences to him. More than one set of guests had already left convinced that they had become *best friends* with the next generation of Adrianakis men.

Yet he called her the actress.

Part of her ached at that, because surely, since they were both so surprisingly good at this, they should have been able to band together. To work *with* each other, not *against* each other. Surely there had to be some way to make themselves a team instead of dire enemies, forever and ever, amen.

But even as she thought that, she felt something bitter twist her lips.

Who was she kidding? She was the too-young woman who had married his father. She should count herself lucky that he was able to maintain the level of civility he already did. Maybe she would have to learn how to be thankful for that.

And besides, she had duties to perform. She couldn't keep hiding out here, not when there was so much at stake. Not when she knew that he would take anything she did and make it negative.

So Jolie welded her smile into place and did what she did best. For years now.

She made herself *indispensable*.

The sun took its time sinking all the way down to the horizon. It stretched out as it went, shooting glorious hues as far as it could reach. Oranges. Pinks. Deep tendrils of violet.

When it was dark at last, the singer was prevailed upon to gift a few songs to the assembly. Everyone gathered around, listening as he played. The first two songs were contemplative. Almost mournful, like quiet elegies into the night as it settled around them.

And once again, Jolie found herself drawn to Apostolis's gaze—only to find that that he was closer now.

He smiled at the person beside him as if they had bonded, soul to soul, and then made his way over to Jolie.

Because, she reminded herself sternly, that was what a married couple *would* do. That was what people were truly intimate did. They went out of their way to be close to each other even when that closeness had nothing to do with sex.

Hadn't she watched her grandparents model this behavior for years?

Jolie thought that it must have been the music that was making her think about her grandparents now. About grief and loss, and how it was woven so tightly into every moment that came after that, perhaps, it became its own complicated tapestry. Made up of joy and despair, because that was what made a life. Without them, what would living be but boring?

Maybe that was why, when she felt that blast of heat beside her that she knew by now was Apostolis, come to stand next to her, she risked tipping back her head to look at him directly.

He was already gazing back down at her. And beneath all the lights that were strung about the pergola, there was no pretending she couldn't see all the different shades of deep, rich, brown and black his eyes were. That bittersweet gleam with something magical shot through it all, as if he was made of the same gold that they'd all watched dance over the waves tonight.

A part of the sun's last breath before it surrendered to the night.

The crowd jostled slightly then and she found herself pressed up against the length of Apostolis's body—in a way that *truly* married people would not mind in the least.

She made herself smile. She made herself laugh a little, as if this was the time of her life, because she needed people to believe it was. That was one of her most important duties.

So she did her best. When he wrapped an arm around her shoulders. When he tucked her up against him so that she was straddling the side of his body. When she was stood there like that, one hand on the front of his chest and the other at his side.

And the fact that they were touching like this in public, paradoxically, seemed to her like the most intimate they had ever been.

Maybe it was because the touching wasn't the point.

They weren't locked up in that carriage house, slugging it out in yet another round of their endless battle. This was the sort of offhanded intimacy that long-term couples accepted as their due. This was the kind of familiarity that simply happened over time and togetherness.

This was as if they actually were the story they pretended they were for the guests.

And when the music changed and the singer began to sing something silkier and more suggestive, it was as if the melody…simply swept them away.

Everyone began to dance. All around them, people

paired up into couples, and then everything was that sway, that silk, that sultry little song. How could she resist?

Jolie didn't.

And it was something perilous and precious indeed to be in Apostolis's arms, then. To have this music to move them, but to be aware of very little else but that look on his face, the heat in his gaze, and the way they fit together so perfectly.

She was not exactly surprised to discover that he was an excellent dancer. She supposed that both of them had been trained for that, one way or another. What surprised her was that it didn't feel in the least bit awkward.

What it felt like, she almost didn't dare think to herself, was that if they could just stop talking—stop sniping, stop looking for weaknesses—they might actually be perfect for each other.

There and then, because *perfect* was too scary to contemplate with a man sworn to destroy her, she decided instead to stop worrying where all this would lead.

It was one night. It was one song.

It was just a dance, that was all.

And though it wasn't a total surrender, she still felt as if that was what she did, here. She surrendered to the music. She surrendered to the sparkling lights up above her and the stars beyond. She surrendered to the lure of the grand hotel and the sultry invitation of the singer's music.

She surrendered to the press of the crowd around her

and the current of joy and excitement that ran through every one of them, at the same time, when the other singers joined in and brought out their own kind of percussion—on tables, with their hands, whatever worked.

And all the while, she and this man who had already claimed more of her than she'd intended to give away, danced and danced and danced.

It was much later, after a leisurely meal, too many drinks, and several more wild, unpredicted dances around the terrace that even the staff joined in, that Jolie finally left the main hotel building to head for the carriage house.

And she wasn't alone.

Apostolis was with her, his arm slung over her shoulder as it had been far too much this night. She could feel the weight of him, pressing into her, making her walk at a different pace. Making her feel as if she was a part of all his heat and lean muscle.

They didn't speak. The night was too hushed all around them. The stars were too close.

He led them over to the door and opened it, then walked her inside without untangling his body from hers.

And then there was that moment. The moment that grew harder and more unwieldy every night. The moment where they had to decide if they would drop their act...or not.

If they would perhaps...let it linger. If there would be a hushed, drawn-out moment—

Usually one of them broke it by starting up the usual hostilities.

But tonight, it didn't seem to work that way. He didn't turn the lights on. She didn't pull away.

They stood there in the shadows of the hall and somehow he had turned her so that she was facing him. They were standing almost as if, at any moment, they might break into a new kind of dance. One that didn't need any music. One that would simply be…theirs.

They were *so close* now. And they had danced so much tonight that she felt she knew him in a whole different way. Her breath began to *hurt* as it moved in and out of her body and she was fairly certain that the pulse she felt inside her skin was his. As if hers matched his completely, making a kind of beat all their own now, too.

"Jolie…" he began.

Normally that would be the start of something. A spark that would quickly flare, and then they could both gain some distance with harsh words, with accusations, with this *thing* between them.

This architecture she was beginning to think was a whole lot of scaffolding disguised to hide a terrible truth. A fragile, impossible swelling of something that was nothing like *hate* at all.

Or even anything as relatively simple as attraction.

It felt a lot more like hope.

And that was why, before he could puncture it, she said something she'd vowed she never would. Certainly not to him. Because she preferred to let him think whatever he liked. Because that said far more about him than it ever could about her.

"My marriage with your father wasn't what you think," she told him.

His breath escaped him in a rush, as if to suggest she might as well have kneed him in the gut. Or lower still.

"This is the conversation you wish to have? Right now?"

She knew she couldn't let him throw gasoline on the kindling she could hear in his voice. Because once he did, when would they feel like this again?

When she thought about it that way, five years felt like an eternity.

"I thought it would be what you imagined it was," she said.

They still hadn't turned the lights on, and that was a help. It encouraged her. She could feel how taut he was as he waited for her to go on. She understood without him having to say a word that she was running out of time. That there was only so much space he would give to whatever stories she wanted to tell him before he moved them back to familiar footing.

"You already know that I met him at your sister's and my graduation," Jolie said. "There were events beforehand, and all that week he paid particular attention to me. So I paid particular attention back. And yes, I had no money. None. My situation was dire and I knew it, but your sister had already invited me to spend the summer here. And I had already accepted, thinking that on an island like this, surely I could find something—or, yes, *someone*—who might be a good prospect for the kind of life I wanted."

"A life of ease and comfort, with your every whim

catered to?" he asked, but very sardonically, because of course he thought he already knew the answer.

"The headmistress had made my situation very clear to me." Jolie found his face in the shadows. "When I said I had no money, I don't mean I had only a little. All I had was the kindness of friends, and you and I both know that people find it very easy to be generous to those who don't appear to need it. And somewhat less easy to be equally generous to those who do need it, especially if their need is obvious. I was grateful for your sister, but I was nervous about what came next. I already knew that it would be difficult to spend a life like that, drifting from friend to friend and then, perhaps, to the questionable kindness of strangers."

"Because a job was out of the question, of course."

"It wasn't out of the question at all," she retorted. "That was actually what I was hoping I could find here."

He shifted against the wall, leaning back and crossing his arms as he regarded her in that narrow, dark way of his. She still couldn't understand why he, out of all the people in the world, could make her *shake* with the need to prove to him that his opinion of her was wrong. "I assume that the moment you arrived here, you raced down into each and every village and put yourself about, shaking the olive trees for employment."

"That would not be effortless, would it?" She said it softly, and though he didn't reply, she could tell he understood what she was getting at. "That was the trouble, of course. I was afraid that if your sister saw how desperate I truly was, she would ask me to leave. I decided to wait for opportunities and then take them where I could. In the meantime, I spent a lot of time with your father."

"I bet you did."

Jolie sighed. "Did it occur to me that he might want to *marry* me? Absolutely not. I assumed that he might be interested in an affair." She sighed, remembering. "He had showed no interest in marrying any of the other women he was linked to over the years. It never occurred to me that he might wish to marry *me*."

"So you thought you could get what you wanted if you just rolled around with him a bit," Apostolis summarized. Witheringly. "Give the old man a little sugar and see if he paid for the pleasure."

She was already regretting the urge that had led to this. "Your sister is actually the one who played match-maker. Dioni thought it would be fun if she got to keep a friend here with her, which wouldn't happen if I was just another affair. They all tend to storm off, sooner or later. So one night she laughed quite loudly while your father was telling me some story, leaned in close, and said, *Father, really. If you're going to captivate my friend's attention every time you see her, why not marry her yourself?*"

Apostolis looked as if he wanted to claim she was lying about Dioni, too.

"I don't know if that was the first time he considered it," Jolie told him. "But I do know that he changed his approach after that. He asked me to marry him that August. And I accepted."

"Of course you accepted. It would be foolish to turn away a meal ticket."

"But this meal ticket is not quite the one you think it was," she made herself tell him, because she'd started this, hadn't she? And there was no point telling only half the story. "After he proposed, and once he understood that I was prepared to accept, he didn't sweep me off for some romantic evening. He sat me down and had a long talk with me about what he wanted. What he demanded of me, and would expect of a wife."

Apostolis's bittersweet gaze flared. "I'm certain he did exactly that, and I'm equally certain that I would rather not hear of it in any detail."

"It's not as lurid as the things I read about you in widely circulated newspapers," she tossed back at him, with more heat than she wanted to show him. She tried to compose herself. "First and foremost, he regretted to inform me that—to his great regret—*that* part of his anatomy was not in service."

Apostolis made a strangled sort of sound. "I... That's not better."

"What he wanted was a daydream. A fantasy. A beautiful young woman on his arm, who could convince the world by her very presence that he was still the man that he liked to see when he looked in the mirror. A pretty girl who could charm his guests, laugh at his jokes, and make him feel like a king for whatever time he had left. He told me he doubted very much that he would make it ten years. I assumed that meant he would last at least fifteen and more probably, twenty." Jolie squared her shoulders. "The only thing he required from me was my assurance that I would never let anyone know the truth. That ours was not the intense, wildly sexual connection he wanted them to think it was. The connection you seem to be sure it was. The connection I think I wanted to pretend it was, too, because that was better than the truth. Better than a *transaction*."

"And…" Apostolis's voice was so soft. But she shivered, because she could hear the menace in it. "Do you expect me to believe that the two of you were simply…*playing charades* for seven years? That my father, who made a point of pushing what he liked to call his *earthiness* on anyone who strayed near, was involved in this…chaste bit of dinner theater? You must think I am the most gullible fool who ever drew breath."

"He was more my boss than my husband." Jolie told him this quietly. "He was not entirely unkind. But both of us knew who was in control. Of everything. Every night he would critique my performance and to be honest with you, I don't think he was very much interested in sex by then. Earthy or otherwise. Not when total control of another person was so much more exciting to have."

That control had even extended to Mathilde, not that she wished to so much as whisper to Apostolis that her cousin existed. But Spyros had been very clear that Jolie was to exist out of time and only for him. He liked that she was an orphan, just as he liked that she was penniless. No family. No connections aside from his own daughter.

He wanted her entirely focused on and dependent upon him.

That she sent money to Mathilde was of no matter to him—but woe betide Jolie if she ever reminded him that her cousin existed. Or that she spent even one moment in his presence thinking of her.

Across from her, Apostolis muttered something dark and very Greek that she found she was perfectly happy not to understand.

"If you think about it, Apostolis," she said in the same low voice, "I'm sure you'll realize that what I'm telling you is the truth. He liked to manipulate people. He liked to watch everyone around him dance to his tune. It didn't matter if it was a happy thing or a sad thing or if they hated it. He just wanted to see what he could make other people do. So it wasn't charades, it was a puppet show. Does that make it better?"

Apostolis ran a hand over his face. Then he let out a dark black laugh that filled the hall, and worse still, filled her as well.

Then he pushed off the wall and came toward her—all of one step, then another.

Her throat seemed to clench tight at that, because he was as close as he could get. Because he was *right here*, and not one part of her body cared how dark the expression on his face was.

What she wanted, more than anything, was to pretend that this was a part of the dancing they'd been doing all night—

Especially when he slid an arm around her waist and hauled her even closer, so she sprawled into his chest and had to prop herself against that hard, muscled wall when all she really wanted was to melt into all his heat and strength.

"Jolie," he murmured. Then he said her name a few times, as if he was chanting it, like some kind of prayer, a breath away from her lips. "I don't believe a word you say."

She jolted, as if he'd tossed her off the cliff and into the sea far below. "But—"

"Not one single word," he said, his voice a rough thread of sound.

And then he closed what distance was left and licked his way to her mouth.

Making everything within her, everything she was, nothing but fire and desire.

It was a punch of need so bright and so hot that it threatened to take her down.

So wild that she was tempted to forget that he could hear the truth from her own lips and doubt it—

He kissed her, then kissed her again, as if he didn't mean to stop.

And she understood that despite everything, she didn't want him to.

Apostolis pressed her back against the wall and held her wrists beside her head, and Jolie arched up against him, exulting in this. In every bit of heat and dark need and wild temptation. As if only when this man held her still did she feel most free.

His mouth moved on her, consuming her, and she knew that she should fight him. That she should push him away and gather up her weapons, point them in his direction and start firing them, one after the next.

She knew that she should handle this the way she'd handled everything since she'd married Spyros. He had called it her *maddening dignity*. He had never come close to piercing it in all their years together.

He had never gotten past her walls.

She had let him play his puppeteer games and had smiled through it all. And never, not ever, had she let him see that he got to her. Jolie couldn't tell if he'd loved her for that or hated her for it, toward the end.

But she didn't know if she had it in her to keep that up. Not with Apostolis.

Not with the man who kissed her like this, as if devouring her whole. The man who could say, straight to her face, that she was a liar and he didn't believe her—then kiss her as if he couldn't bear the thought of another breath without the taste of her in his mouth.

This was the one game she didn't know how to play.

So she kissed him back.

And she told herself it wasn't *hope* that swelled in her, but that fascination that—if she was scrupulously honest—she'd always felt toward him. From the very start, there had been something about the way Apostolis disliked her. The way he'd made sure she knew it.

This dynamic between them had always excited her.

She could admit that tonight.

And she had five years of this ahead of her. She had told him the truth, he didn't believe it, and now there was this.

She kissed him back, their tongues started their own

war, and this time she knew that there was no winning. That either way, win or lose or draw, it was the same thing—and maybe it needed to end up naked. Maybe it had always needed to go straight to bed.

Maybe this was seven years overdue.

So when he swept her up into his arms and carried her up the stairs, then down the hall to his bedroom— where she had refused to set foot—she let him.

Because if she couldn't have *hope*, she might as well have *him*.

In whatever way she could manage.

CHAPTER EIGHT

HE DIDN'T BELIEVE a word she said.

But this last, best battlefield did not require words. Words had done their worst. Now there was only the enduring truth of this connection he was certain neither one of them wished to feel.

The time for wishes was past, too.

He spread her out on his bed, aware of a great, glowing thing inside of him—as if the fact of her presence alone set alight something in him he wasn't sure he could identify. It made sense, he assured himself. Once he had reluctantly accepted that there was no way out of this marriage, he had always assumed that this moment would come. Sooner or later.

Now it was here.

Apostolis could taste her in his mouth. And her kiss had been a revelation, again.

And now he had to wrestle with that great glow within, the greedy demands of his sex, and the simple fact that he had wanted her almost *too* long.

They all crowded together inside of him, as if jostling for position.

If he was someone else, Apostolis thought, he might

well have found himself paralyzed now that this moment had arrived.

But he felt as if he'd spent his whole life getting ready for this. For her.

Jolie pushed herself up onto her elbows, shaking back that golden hair that he thought about far more often than he should. He did not let himself think too much about the things she'd told him, and not only because he didn't believe her.

But because the very last thing he wished to think about just now was his father.

Or anyone else, for any reason.

Something that might have alarmed him under different circumstances.

"Are you having second thoughts?" she asked, back to that arch, mocking voice of hers that he found still set him on fire. As if he needed more encouragement to let the flames in him reach high. "Or is it..." She smiled, benevolently, which between them was akin to a sword strike. "It's all right. It happens to everyone from time to time, or so I hear. Despite their best intentions, they just can't manage to make the equipment work."

"I think," he said as he crawled onto the bed and sprawled himself out beside her, at last, "that I'm finished with all of this *talking*, Jolie."

Before she could argue about that—because he knew that she would argue about that—he set his mouth to hers once more.

And this time it seemed impossible that anything, even the end of the world itself, would stop them.

Apostolis would see to it personally.

He kissed her again and again, taking note of when she kissed him back even more fiercely. Of how and when her lips clung to his. Or how and when she became more urgent, more demanding, pressing her body into his until he let her push him over to his back so he could hold her above him, feeling her body all over his, and this time, not while dancing on a terrace packed full of people.

This dance was far more intimate. And only his.

Her hands moved over him the way they had once before. But this time he could also feel the press of her soft breasts as she unbuttoned his shirt, tracking her way down the length of his chest until she could shove aside the sides of his linen shirt and bury her face between.

She made a low noise of pleasure, as if she'd been waiting to do that for a very long time.

He stopped her when she got to his trousers, hauling her up again then sitting up as he set her astride him. So he could help himself to the hem of the gown she wore and peel it up and then off her body, revealing her to him at last.

It was different than the times he'd seen her by the pool or sunning herself on a boat, in even the skimpiest bikini.

It was different because he was touching her this time. And she was spread open before him like an exquisite feast.

Best of all, the hardest part of him was pressed into

the V of her thighs, and he got to watch the way the feel of him against her softest parts made her sigh.

Her eyes when they found his were so blue it hurt.

But this was the kind of pain Apostolis enjoyed.

Indulging the first of a series of near-ungovernable urges, he sank his hands deep into her hair. And allowed himself, for a moment, to catalog nothing.

To *feel,* first and foremost.

Because her hair was a warm silk, flowing over his hands. And when he curled his fingers, her head angled back, giving him access to the fine line of her throat. He skated his lips over her jaw, then found the throb of her pulse.

And he wasn't sure which one of them groaned as she moved her hips against him, but the pleasure that shot through him was almost too intense to bear. Apostolis was certain it was the same for her.

Keeping one hand buried in all that hair, he used his other hand to smooth its way to the jut of her breasts, reaching between them to snap open the fastener to her bra. He tossed it aside and then, at last, helped himself to the plump curves he had only imagined before. He used his thumb to gently abrade one nipple while he set his mouth to the other. And he made sounds of appreciation as she melted against him, arching her back the way he'd imagined she would—to press her breasts into his mouth, his hand.

To stoke the fire that burned white-hot in both of them.

She was rocking herself against him, making greedy little noises in the back of her throat with every tug on each of her proud nipples. And Apostolis felt the exact moment that she stiffened—

Then cried out as she began to shake against him.

Losing herself so completely that he actually questioned, for a too-long moment—if he could keep himself under control.

And he still had his trousers on.

He held her as she shook, whispering nonsense words in Greek as he kissed his way back up the length of her body, and combed his fingers through her hair again. He moved it back from that flawless face of hers, marveling at her beauty the way he always did.

But tonight he admired her fire even more.

And when she opened her eyes to look at him again, her eyes were a shade of blue so brilliant he should have been blinded.

Apostolis thought he felt a kind of scar begin to form, deep inside him.

He kissed her again, slowly. Deeply.

Taking his time, and mindful of that scar and her fire, he began to pour all the intensity and tension inside of him into her mouth. He rolled her over while he did it, so he could set himself to the sweet task of stripping the panties she wore from her body, a filmy little bit of lace that he tossed aside.

This time, when he made his way down her body, he gave her gorgeous breasts only the most cursory attention before he traveled on. He enjoyed the indentation of her waist before her hips flared out again. He took a detour to the shallow delight that was her navel.

And then, at last, making his way down between

her legs, he found that she was even prettier than he'd expected she would be, lush and ready.

She was shaking, though it was not the same kind of *shaking apart* as before, more's the pity.

"Apostolis—"

But something was growling in him as he shifted her legs wide open so he could wedge his shoulders in between her thighs. He let her legs dangle there over his back, and then he bent down, slid his hands over the sweet, soft curves of her bottom, and wasted no time licking his way deep into her. As if he was trying to eat her alive.

Maybe he was.

Because there were no words, there was only this.

The sweet truth of who she was. The salt of her, the tart delight.

The way she lifted herself to meet his mouth. The way her shaking changed again to something more rhythmic, a sultry circle of her hips. When he glanced up, she looked like a goddess. Her arms were thrown back over her head, her back was arched up, and her lips were parted as if she couldn't quite take in the glory of what was happening.

Neither could he.

Apostolis built this fire carefully and thoroughly.

And when he was ready, he threw a little gas on it, using his teeth against her most sensitive center, and she screamed.

Jolie bucked against him as she shook on and on and on.

He rolled from the bed, stripping his clothes from

his body and more than a little surprised to find that his own hands betrayed the slightest bit of unsteadiness. As if he was as affected as she was.

As if, something in him whispered, *you're not in control of this at all.*

But there was no time to worry about things like that, not when she was naked and still quivering on his bed.

And this time, when he crawled onto the bed beside her, he tucked her beneath him. He propped himself up on his elbows, settled between her legs, and finally pressed the hardest part of him into all that sweet softness that he could still taste on his lips.

That he imagined he would always taste, always yearn for, always dream of—like the ghost of her was forming all around him as they breathed like this, together.

Her eyes were dreamy and lost. And he watched as awareness took her over, as her body shifted and flushed as she felt all that heat and thickness that waited there for her.

What he hoped she did not understand was that he was holding on to his control by the slimmest of threads.

Her breath shuddered out of her. She slid her hands up to hold on to his neck.

And Apostolis expected her to say something cutting now. To bring this back to the ground he knew well.

Jolie didn't say a word. It was all blue eyes and that same expectant wildfire that burned in him, too.

And so, feeling less *triumphant* than he expected to

and something far more like *reverent,* he thrust deep into his wife. His stepmother.

His, something in him asserted.

But she sucked in a harsh breath. And he felt the way her body flinched beneath him.

Apostolis froze.

Her eyes were closed, squeezed tight, and he waited without moving even an inch, aware of every single place she was clenched too tight.

"Breathe," he told her quietly. Intently. "I apologize. I didn't realize it had been so long for you."

Slowly, carefully, he felt her settle beneath him. Only when she released the nails she'd dug into the back of his neck did he even understand that she'd pierced him in the first place.

But it wasn't until she opened up her eyes that he relaxed, just slightly.

"Jolie," he began, but stopped dead.

Because the way she was looking at him…

Her eyes were wide, and too bright with what he could not pretend he didn't know were unshed tears. And she said not one word.

Still, he understood.

Her tightness. Her tenseness. One small breath when anyone else might have screamed, and no matter that she'd found her pleasure twice already.

He couldn't believe it.

He didn't *want* to believe it.

"You are a virgin," he said, a flat statement of fact.

She closed her eyes for another moment, giving him entirely too much time to wonder how anyone's eyelashes could be so long, so thick. When she opened them again, the brightness that had been so ripe with tears was gone.

But there was still a softness there that hadn't been there before.

A vulnerability he had not known she possessed.

That scar she'd left in him began to throb, as if it was lengthening, and cutting him deep.

He pulled back, slowly, and then thrust in again, so gentle it almost undid him. But he was focused on her. He watched her pull in a breath, then sigh it out a little.

And he felt the rest of her quiver.

Slightly, but it was there.

"I am told the pain is fleeting," he said. "We will make sure that it is."

"Are we a *we* now?" she asked softly, in a thick voice that sounded nothing like the Jolie he knew. "How lucky that there is physical proof that I'm exactly who I told you I was. No need for you to believe me in any act of faith. No need for you to concern yourself with the reasons why you might be predisposed to distrust me. You can just—"

"Quiet," he whispered. "You do not have to take every opportunity to fight me, Jolie. Especially not now."

And when she looked as if she might continue arguing, he kissed her.

It was different from before. It was...seeking.

Penitent, perhaps.

He kissed her over and over while holding himself

perfectly still, so that when there was movement again, it was hers.

And he felt something far too close to relief in every slow, incremental movement she made against him. Moving her hips this way, then that. Lifting herself up, then lowering her hips once more.

Slowly, carefully, he let her learn him. He let her find her way back to pleasure.

He let her work herself into a new fire of her own making until she was frowning, not quite complaining, but digging her fingernails into him as if that could make him move with her.

When he did, when he finally took over and set a deep, hard rhythm, she came apart almost instantly.

Still he held himself back, keeping that same, steady, maddeningly slow pace. She flew apart again and then she was back, and wilder. Her eyes too wide and much too blue.

And she knew, now, how to meet his thrusts. How to prolong the drag, then strike sparks with the pump.

She was a marvel, and she was his.

Only and ever his.

And it was that thought, he was certain, that had him breaking from his rhythm. That let his hips find their own intensity as he threw her over the cliff once more.

Only then, at last, did he allow himself to follow.

Only then did he lose himself completely.

It was much later, well into the dark of the night, when she finally stirred beside him again. They had still not turned on a single light in the house and so it was only the moon, rising high outside the windows, that illuminated his bed.

And the way she looked at him was something like shy.

Once again, too many words and too many weapons crowded into him, making him feel tangled up with it all, but he ignored it.

He picked her up, enjoying the silk slide of her skin against his. In the bathroom, he still didn't turn on any lights. He took her into his expansive shower and set her on the bench. He set the water pressure and the heat, and then he took his place on the bench, too, so that she was seated between his widespread legs, leaning back against his chest.

Then he took his time washing her. Taking care with her body. Worshiping her in an entirely different way.

And when he found traces of her virgin's blood upon her thighs, he washed it away, murmuring words of regret as he did it.

But in Greek, which he wasn't sure she entirely understood.

He risked a glance at her, leaning back against his chest with her face tipped up toward him, and found the glint of those clever blue eyes of hers.

"No need to parade the sheets through the village, then," she murmured. "Lucky me. Or do I mean lucky you?"

A phalanx of retorts lined up inside him, but he tamped them back down. "I would think that you would be pleased that you possessed, this whole time, the

CAITLIN CREWS 151

means to prove yourself. What I do not understand is why you did not use it sooner."

"Because I shouldn't have to prove myself to you," she said, but quietly. "Or anyone."

"You would prefer that I continue to think the worst of you?"

"Apostolis." She breathed out his name in a way that made him think she liked to taste it as much as he liked hers. Her gaze laughed at him, though she did not smile. "I already know the truth. That doesn't change. So what does it matter what you think of me?"

He felt that glowing thing inside of him swell once more. And he didn't like the way her question made him feel, so he shifted, letting her head fall back on his shoulder so he could kiss her once more.

But she laughed as she pushed him away, and surprised him by turning around so she could straddle him on the bench.

"Maybe you should ask yourself why it is that nature did not provide men with a similar, handy little lie detector test. Is it that men are more trustworthy? Or less, rendering everything they say moot before they say it?"

"I am not the liar here."

"While I am sure you will find a way to make sure that I still am," she replied. "Now that I cannot use my innocence to shame you."

But then, to his surprise, she reached down between them and busied herself with stroking the length of him.

Already at attention, he grew harder, thicker at her

touch, and then had to grip the edge of his seat as she rocked up on her knees and guided him into her heat once more.

And then she took them both on a wild, glorious ride that had them both shouting out their pleasure as the hot water pounded down all around them in the dark of his shower.

It was much later when he found himself wide awake, staring at the moonlight that fell across his room and caught at all her blond hair as she lay there, tucked up beneath his arm.

As if she had always been meant to fit just like that.

Apostolis found he was having trouble breathing. There was a tight band across his chest and it had nothing to do with the arm she'd thrown over him.

Jolie had been a virgin. She had been a *virgin,* and that meant so many things that he was almost reluctant to look at.

The band around him pulled tighter and tighter.

It got no looser as the night wore on.

He held her as she slept and found himself going over every single interaction they had ever had, looking for clues that this was possible. How had he missed it? How had he misread her so completely?

By the time the sun rose over another perfect blue-and-gold day, he had moved over to the window. He heard her stir in the bed behind him and turned, rubbing a hand over his chest to make sure that the last of that band that had clamped so tight all night had finally loosened its hold on him.

He was relieved to find that it had. Because he had discovered the solution.

Jolie sat up, pushing all that hair back from her face. That wild blue gaze of hers settled on him warily.

He watched her, aware of a kind of spiraling fury that rose in him, because she was still so damned *beautiful*. She still looked like a dream, every dream he'd had. A bit of tousled elegance in his bed after such a long night.

It was entirely possible that this woman was going to be the death of him.

But if that was true, he had every intention of taking her with him.

And he had five years to work on the perfect exit strategy.

That wariness in her gaze intensified when all he did was stare at her.

But if he expected her to let the tears he'd seen in her gaze the night before take her over again, he was mistaken. He'd expected her to cringe away, but she sat up instead.

Until she was very much giving the impression that he was the one currying her favor here.

He expected her to say something. Anything. Instead, she waited. And did not pull the sheet up over herself, but simply sat there, the glory of her lovely body on display.

He suspected she knew that very well.

Perhaps he was not the only one who woke determined to find new weapons.

"I was up all night castigating myself," he told her.

"Were you?" She tilted her head slightly to one side as she considered him. "You seem to have come through it well enough."

"I could not imagine how it was that I could have thought you so wicked when all this time, you were as pure as the driven snow in every respect."

Perhaps wisely, she did not respond.

"But then," he said softly and with intent, "after I sifted through what I know to be true and all the many stories you've told me over time, I remembered."

"That your father was a monster and he made everyone in his orbit miserable?" she asked lightly. "Isn't that what you said to me once?"

"That is a foregone conclusion." He moved closer to the bed so he could stand above her. Or maybe he just liked it when she had to tip her head back like that to look at him. Maybe there was something in him that took entirely too much joy in how defiantly she looked at him, even now. "But that does not explain the *money,* does it."

He had the satisfaction of watching a kind of electric shock go through her at that.

At last, he thought with great satisfaction, they were back on familiar ground.

"Nothing to say?" he taunted her in a low voice. "No explanation?" He shook his head as if her response made him sad, when it was the opposite. "I suppose I will have to hunt these answers down myself."

Jolie surged up, coming onto her knees, and she was flushed once again. With temper, he supposed, though he liked that much better than the unbearable notion that he had *hurt* her.

She pointed a finger directly into his face and she did not waver as she made an entirely anatomically impossible suggestion of what he could do with his anatomy.

In her clearest, coldest, most outrageously *serene* voice.

"Tempting," Apostolis murmured, and then he hauled her up and into his arms. "When this is so much easier. No yoga positions required."

And then he bore her back down onto the bed and threw them right back into the heat of their battle.

CHAPTER NINE

EVERYTHING CHANGED.

Again.

This time, the world ending and yet beginning again felt to Jolie as if she was trapped inside some kind of dream. Long, golden days, impossibly blue skies, and these hot, impossible nights that seemed to last whole lifetimes.

She had thought she understood sex. What it was, anyway. And she'd imagined how it would feel.

What she discovered was that while she understood the *performance* of it, the *suggestion* of it, she knew nothing about the *reality* of sex. Because real sexual intimacy was almost shocking in its intensity. It created vulnerability. Impossible need. It was raw, unpredictable, and had far-reaching ramifications that she wasn't certain she'd even fully discovered yet.

She felt as if she could feel them, rumbling along beneath her like new fault lines she'd never understood were there before, lurking. Waiting for the opportunity to shake apart everything she thought she was. Everything she *wanted* to be.

On the one hand, life at the Andromeda went on the way it always had.

Jolie performed her typical duties. She was the same smiling, endlessly accommodating hostess, going out of her way to appear to do very little while making certain that everything was in its place. That all the details were *just so*. Out of sight of the guests, she and Apostolis would sit down together in the office and talk about numbers, accounts both payable and receivable, staff and vendor issues, and all the rest of the things that fell to both of them to handle now.

Whenever they were in public—or anywhere that they could not be completely certain of their privacy— they would play their happy, newlywed games for the benefit of their guests and the hotel's enduring legacy.

Only now, when they went back to the carriage house, they imploded.

It was like fireworks.

They rarely made it three steps into the house before they were tearing off each other's clothes. Before they were climbing on each other, licking and biting and digging their fingers into each other's flesh, as if they weren't quite certain if they wanted to feast on each other or simply ride out the sensation.

It was always impossibly perfect, the glory and raw intensity of the things they did to each other.

She learned that despite what she'd imagined all this time thanks to images she'd seen or things she'd read, she actually loved kneeling down before him. She loved taking him in her mouth, and listening to the noises that she could make him let out.

As if she was not the only one who could be torn into pieces in this fire of theirs.

She found that she loved the taste of him, the salt of his skin, the richness that was all man and entirely Apostolis.

There was nothing she did not allow him. There in the dark of the carriage house, it was as if the pair of them were made of nothing but flesh and need.

And if it was harder, every morning, to pull herself together and back into one piece again, she supposed she should have expected that. For surely there could not be such exquisite pleasure, and so much of it, without a price.

"It's called hate sex," he told her one night as he moved deep inside her body from behind, his hands gripping her hips as he plunged again and again. "And just think, my darling wife—we have years of this ahead of us."

The very idea had made her shatter into pieces, there and then.

Afterward, she lay awake in the bed they now shared, tangled up in him in more ways than one. And she wondered how it was possible to survive like this. If she would make it—because it seemed impossible to her that these were the kind of storms that anyone could actually live through.

But then again, she had to. She had no choice. There was someone else to consider beyond these wild passions and besides, she had already come so far. There could be no going back.

Yet as time went on, funnily enough, it wasn't the long, explosive nights that she feared might break her.

It was the performance of a very different relationship than the once they actually had that they put on, night after night.

It was the way he gazed at her across the table filled with their guests. It was the way he put his arm on the back of her chair and let his thumb gently stroke the bare flesh of her shoulder.

It was the way they danced, now and again, as if the whole of the starry sky above them was nothing next to the flame that moved between them.

She found herself making up stories about the two different lives they led, all wrapped up and tangled into this one.

Maybe he was as astonished by it as she was. Maybe he had not expected this kind of connection either.

She told herself that it was more than likely that they were both as shocked by this as she was. That they were both humbled and exalted and made new, one day at a time.

But she didn't dare ask him, no matter what she told herself.

"I keep expecting to hear that the Andromeda has been reduced to rubble," Dioni said on one of their infrequent phone calls. "Or that you've both incinerated each other into a crisp or something equally dramatic, and there's nothing but a crater left behind."

Her friend didn't sound like herself. And Jolie didn't want to ask, because surely Dioni would tell her if she wanted to. She had to pick her way through these fraught and strained conversations, but that was better than not talking to Dioni at all.

"The Andromeda still stands," she said, with a laugh. "You have my word."

"That's a good thing," her friend turned stepdaughter turned sister-in-law said, and there was the sound of something clanging in the background. Like a cafetière being stirred too roughly with a metal spoon. "Are you happy?"

Jolie longed to tell Dioni the truth. Or some part of the truth. She wanted nothing more than to unburden herself, to open up and lay out for her friend every single thing that had happened since she'd left the island.

But she couldn't.

Because Dioni looked up to Apostolis. He was, in many ways, her own, personal god. He was the one who had taken care of her when she was small. He was the one she'd run to. Dioni had told Jolie all of this long before Jolie had ever met him.

And, of course, she had never actually met the Apostolis Dioni knew. That was a gift he gave only to his sister.

The Apostolis Jolie knew had always been little more than a wildfire.

How could Jolie possibly tell Dioni, who thought her brother nothing short of a hero, that he was—in fact—simply a man?

A maddening, glorious, impossible man.

How could she explain to her innocent friend what it was like between them without tarnishing him in Dioni's eyes?

Jolie found she couldn't do it.

It was far better for Dioni to imagine that Jolie and Apostolis had sorted things out in the wake of their contentious wedding, and were now...reasonably content.

"I am no expert on happiness," she told her friend now. "But every day dawns no matter what went on the day before, and that feels like a gift. The sun rises and when it sets again, I have very little to complain about."

Dioni laughed from all the way across two seas. "What an ode to joy. You should open up a business in inspirational talks. Perhaps a line of greeting cards?"

"Are *you* happy?" Jolie asked her in return.

She heard Dioni pulling in a breath. "I am an Adrianakis," she said after a moment. "Happiness is in our blood. Ask anyone who's ever visited the Andromeda. Happiness is a requirement of residence."

And Jolie sat on the window seat in the room she now shared with Apostolis for some time after they both rang off, frowning out at the place where the blue sky met a deeper blue sea.

Because neither one of them had answered the question, had they?

Still, she resolved to take it as a challenge. What she'd said to Dioni was true enough, or not a lie, anyway. She had nothing to complain about. She had decided to sleep with her husband. She had allowed it this time when he'd had the staff move her things back into this bedroom. She did not see it as a concession, but a *choice*.

That being so, why shouldn't she be happy about it?

Whether it was *hate sex* or not, the sex that she and Apostolis were having was extraordinary. She might not know the difference, but she had never heard stories that came close to the things they made each other feel. Every time they finished, he looked at her in the same wild astonishment. Sometimes he murmured revealing things into her ear.

You will be the death of me, he liked to say. *I do not think we will survive this.*

How can you be real? he had asked last night.

In Greek, which she still pretended not to understand.

Not because she wanted to deceive him—though she didn't much mind if she did, to be clear. Not where language was concerned. But because she had discovered long ago that if she affected a charming inability to only mangle Greek, people found that delightful. It made them think she was silly. A little bit foolish. It allowed all of the guests, and even the villagers, to feel more comfortable around her.

Jolie knew that many women felt that they should not have to minimize themselves for any reason whatsoever. But she was far more sanguine. She liked any weapon she could find.

And as the days rolled on, one into the next with only the odd bit of weather to distinguish between them, the things he whispered grew more intense.

This is untenable. You are impossible.

Every night they seemed to reach a new and different kind of intensity. They did not necessarily speak to each other. They did not *discuss* the fire they danced in and through.

But Jolie often thought that the way they looked at each other left scars behind.

She could feel them forming all over her, both when they were in private and when they were playing their besotted roles of the newly wedded couple for the guests.

Sometimes he would take her hand and brush a kiss over her knuckles, and everything inside of her would go still, then quiver into goose bumps.

And she would feel it inside her, carving its way into her like every touch was a blade. It marked her just the same.

Those were the sorts of night when the people around the table would talk about their relationship in such disarming, magical phrases that she found herself believing the things they said. Even when she knew better. Even when she knew the truth.

"My wife is a beautiful woman," Apostolis told a group of riveted guests one night. "This goes without saying. But she was married to my father for many years and my appreciation of her beauty was akin to that I have for the hotel itself." He waved a hand at the Andromeda, bearing her graceful witness all around them. "And we take pleasure in that, Jolie and I." The look he gave her was so warm. So bright with love and passion that it made reality seem to slip for her, or perhaps the trouble was, she wished it would slip and then stay. "Because if we had ever seen each other truly before, we could not trust each other now. We would always wonder."

"There is nothing more important than trust," one of the guest sighed happily.

"Sometimes," Apostolis said quietly, "the most marvelous things are hiding in plain sight."

Jolie had always prided herself on the armor she'd learned to wear over the years. But it was her heart that was betraying her now. The poor heart she'd thought was too broken to function after her grandfather died was still there, it seemed.

And it wasn't tough enough for whatever game this was.

Despite her best efforts, it kept on *hoping*.

She found herself sitting on the terrace of the Andromeda, night after night, laughing with this or that collection of shining, resplendent people who loved to come here and gleam out into the Mediterranean. Every night was another bit of brightness, making her feel lit up as if the stars themselves had found their way inside her—even though she knew that they would turn those stars inside out later.

Every sweet moment, every loving gesture, every hint that there were all these beautiful emotions between them had a price.

And Apostolis was a master at exacting those prices, each and every night.

She would forget, all the same. Or she would wrap it all up in the same big bow. Or her foolish heart would beat too hard, because all she could think, more and more with each passing day, was…*what if?*

What if they really could love each other the way they pretended they did?

What if the truth of them was somewhere between the romantic stories they told the enraptured guests about a couple who was not quite them and what he called *hate sex,* which she had never found *hateful* at all?

What if all his talk of *trust* was an olive branch? She, after all, had been the one married to his father. Maybe it was up to her to extend one herself.

Once she started thinking that way, it was the only thing she could think, as if every shuddering beat of her hopeless heart was forcing her to hold nothing else in her head.

It might have scared her if it didn't feel so good.

"You seem distracted today," he said one morning as they waited for the staff to gather for the usual new guest rundown. He eyed her with a certain knowing heat. "Perhaps it is because you screamed yourself hoarse last night, poor thing."

He did not sound the least bit apologetic.

Jolie could feel her cheeks flush as the memories of last night's intensity swept through her, though by now she should have been free of any maidenly blushes. The way he took her apart was so comprehensive that it was a wonder she had any modesty left in her at all.

Then again, it was possible that the way she flushed had nothing to do with shame and everything to do with anticipation. Because every night was only a day away.

Her heart thumped at her, urging her on. "I was just thinking..." she began.

But all her years of necessary and prudent self-preservation kicked in then, hard.

It was as effective as a hand over her mouth. Her pulse sped up. Her whole body tensed.

Was she really ready to risk everything? On a man who had risked nothing at all?

"I prefer it when you are incapable of thought, my darling wife," Apostolis murmured in that dark way that never failed to shower her in sparks, and she wasn't sure if she was grateful or despairing when the staff began to assemble to help create the service profile that would help their new guests imagine that the Andromeda anticipated and exceeded their every need and fancy.

But the urge to tell him things she shouldn't didn't go anywhere.

What she couldn't decide was whether she wanted to tell him for the right reasons. Did she truly believe that she could trust him? Or was she trying to get ahead of the other shoe that she knew he was holding in reserve, so that he could drop it on her when she least expected it?

After all, he was the one who'd brought up the money she paid her aunt and uncle that first night they'd slept together. He hadn't brought it up again since. She would have been very grateful indeed if she'd thought that he'd forgotten it.

She tried to remind herself that he hadn't. That *of*

course he hadn't. And more, he had never given her the slightest reason to imagine he might let anything go.

But her heart kept *thumping* at her all the same.

That night Apostolis got caught up talking to one of the guests as the night was drawing to a close, so Jolie walked over to the carriage house on her own. As that hadn't happened in a while, she indulged herself. She tipped her head back to let the stars shine all over her. She breathed in the sea air. The she let herself into the hall, switched on the lights, and found herself examining the photographs once more. The wall that was a march of time and lives, or whatever it was that such captured moments were so many years and lives later. Unknowable without context. Changeable according to memory or the stories told about them.

She looked at each of them, wondering what was performance and what was real, and carried on down the hall until one caught at her.

It was a picture of Apostolis down on the beach at the foot of the cliff where the hotel stood, holding tight to the hand of a little girl. Dioni.

He could not have been more than twelve in the picture. Dioni was still a toddler. He was looking down at her with so much obvious affection that it never failed to make Jolie's treacherous heart beat a little faster. Years ago, when she'd first seen it, she'd assumed her reaction was because she'd always wanted the kind of older brother Dioni said that Apostolis was to her.

She'd always wanted *someone.* Anyone.

Instead, she supposed, she'd found a way to be

that person for Mathilde. As best she could from so far away.

But this picture hit her differently, now. She had heard a great deal about Apostolis before she ever met him. He had been one of Dioni's favorite topics of conversation in school. Years before she'd met Spyros, Jolie had heard all about this big brother of Dioni's who was her champion in all things—notably unlike her disinterested father.

Apostolis is my hero, Dioni had said, time and again.

When she heard the door to the carriage house open behind her she turned and tried to look at him as if he was *that* Apostolis.

Not the bane of her existence.

Not her enemy.

Not the man she'd married despite the fact he had always been both of those things to her. The man who treated her like someone incalculably precious to him in public and told her he hated her in private, all the while making certain that they were more intimate with each other than she'd had any idea two people *could* be.

Those were all contradictions.

But then, what in life was not? All she had, all anyone ever had, was faith—however misguided—that if they picked one of the many paths available before them, they would be heading in the right direction.

Her heart was a catapult against her ribs.

"I want to talk to you," she said, as he started toward her.

He didn't stop moving, though she thought that the expression on his face grew…more forbidding, perhaps.

Jolie took one last look at that picture of Dioni and him on the beach. Then she moved ahead of him, flicking on every light she passed, perhaps because she wished to signal to him that this was different from their normal late-evening activities.

She moved through the flowing spaces, one into the next in a tumble of bright colors, and found her way to one of the comfortable chairs. And was aware as she sat down that she was choosing it precisely because it did not invite him to sit down with her.

Jolie had no doubt whatsoever that he was receiving all of these messages loud and clear. She could see it in the slight narrowing of his dark, brooding eyes.

"I don't know what you imagine we could have to talk about," he said.

She watched as he prowled around the room, fixing himself a drink at the bar, though he didn't taste it. He only rattled the ice cubes around in his glass tumbler and then lifted a brow in her direction. She shook her head, declining the offer of a drink for herself.

As if she needed to make herself feel even more precarious than she already did, after all the lovely wine she'd sipped at dinner.

"You can't imagine anything at all we might discuss?" she asked, almost idly. Almost in the way she asked questions of all their guests. "How curious. I can think of a number of subjects without even trying."

"I thought we agreed that time is behind us." He roamed closer, then sat in the chair opposite her. Only he sprawled out in such a way that he seemed to take up the entire flowing ground floor that easily. "We have different weapons now. Different battles entirely."

"This has nothing to do with your war," Jolie said, feeling something like exhausted, suddenly. That had to be why emotion seemed to be poking at the back of her eyes. Moving all through her and making her chest feel tight. She pressed her palm against her heart as of that might keep it from beating so hard.

He stared at that hand a long while. Then lifted his brooding gaze to her face. "Nothing that occurs between us is about anything else."

Jolie sighed. "Then you can view this as another attack, if you wish. I've decided to try a radical approach, Apostolis." And it wasn't that her self-preservation instincts had deserted her. She could feel them, kicking at her, as hard as ever. It was that on the other side of that were the things that he whispered to her in the dark. All those gruff, Greek words he thought she couldn't understand. And it was all these bright, golden nights of *maybes*. All these intoxicating *what ifs*. "After all, one of us has to be brave."

He swirled his drink around in its glass. "You think that bravery is involved in these games we play?"

"I think that bravery is required to make certain that we are not playing games any longer," she said quietly. "Aren't you tired of them? I know I am. So I've decided to tell you where that money goes."

She didn't know what she expected. For him to go still, perhaps. To take on that watchful look he sometimes did.

But instead, he seemed to go...*incandescent* instead.

It wasn't that he moved. It wasn't that he roared up out of his chair, like some kind of Roman candle.

But she watched him implode all the same.

"Have you now."

It was all he said, but Jolie could almost taste the bitterness. It seemed a decent match for the color of his gaze as he stared her down.

And it wasn't brave if she quailed at the first hurdle, was it? She forced herself to go on. "A few years after I married your father, the relatives who helped themselves to the estate that my grandfather left me got in touch. They were looking for a handout, naturally. Philosophically, I will say that I find it interesting that the people who steal things can never seem to hold onto them. It's almost as if they know that it was never theirs to begin with."

"Philosophically," he replied in a low, dark tone of voice, "that is a remarkably interesting position for you, of all people, to take."

Jolie chose not to take the bait.

"I wanted very much to encourage them to go to hell," she told him. "But I couldn't. I don't care what happens to the pair of them. When I look back, it isn't even the money that upsets me. It's the fact that they destroyed all the memories I had of my parents. And my grandparents."

She thought of the pictures in the hall. Moments that could change for her depending on who she was when she looked at them again. Moments that could have different meanings over time. That was what her aunt and uncle had stolen from her—that ongoing conversation with still images. That ongoing communion with those stories over time.

But Apostolis's gaze was getting darker by the moment so she kept going. "They sold it all or they threw it out, and the only thing that's left of the people I loved the most in this world is me." She shook her head. "That's the part I find unforgivable."

"You forgive theft, however." His tone was scathing. "What a fascinating morality."

"It's not that I forgive it. It's that, in the fullness of time, what haunts me about that situation isn't what I had to do to survive it, but what I must grieve because of their carelessness. Their greed. There is a distinction."

"If you say so."

But if anything, he looked...thunderous.

"The trouble is that they have a daughter," she said, and she could feel everything inside her revolt. As if her own body would fight her to keep this in, but she was resolved. "Her name is Mathilde. I've only met her once in person, but we have kept in contact ever since." She blew out a breath, because this was more difficult than she'd anticipated and she had expected it to be an uphill climb. "She texts me. That's how I know she's okay. Our deal has always been simple. I pay them off. And they...treat her well."

"You doubt this."

"I think they wouldn't know how to treat a piece of garbage well," Jolie said, more sharply than she'd meant to. "Much less a girl. But I have insisted that they educate her as I was educated. I have insisted that they do not treat her the way they treated me. Or worse." She searched his face, wanting to implore him, but somehow sensing that he would not be open to it. "Do you understand? I had to keep her safe. That's what I've been doing. And I need to continue to do it for the next few years, until I am free and can help her myself. In person."

And for an eternity, or possibly more, they only sat there like this.

His gaze on hers like a hammer.

"So let me make certain that I'm understanding this story," he said at the dawn of what must have been the tenth eternity. "It is richly detailed, and yet, somehow, it is missing some critical information."

Her chest hurt. "I don't think that it is."

"You met this girl once, but she has somehow become the center of your life."

Jolie eyed him. "Not everyone is like you, Apostolis. Some of us do not treat every interaction like a transaction, with prices to be paid at a time of your choosing. It's hard to imagine, I know."

"This is the daughter of two villains, according to your telling, yet you have somehow assumed responsibility for her. In a way that many parents do not assume responsibility for their own children."

"It's called empathy," she said quietly. Because it was that or shout. Or scream. Or worst of all, sob. "I can't say that I expect you to know the feeling, but I would have thought that you'd heard of it."

"But why?" He asked the question too softly. It made

a kind of warning shoot along her spine. "There are so many lost girls in the world. Why this one?"

"Why...?" That warning shot through her again, but she had started down this path. She had to keep going. She had to see it to the end—and she wasn't sure why she felt that so keenly. As if this was a *do or die* situation. "I suppose she reminds me a little bit too much of me."

"Now it makes sense. Narcissism, I can believe."

Jolie shot to her feet, surprised to find that she was shaking. "You don't have to believe anything that I say. I don't know what possessed me to imagine that you might. But Mathilde is all there is, Apostolis. She's the last secret I'm holding onto." When he only stared back at her in that same way, she shook her head. "Now you know everything. And look at you, you're even angrier than before."

"I'm not angry. I just don't believe you."

And it cost her more than she wanted to admit to keep her voice calm. "It's almost as if you're afraid that if you did believe me, this whole fantasy world that you've built up will come crumbling down."

"Do I live in a fantasy world?" Apostolis laughed, and it was not a pleasant sound. "I rather thought that it was a prison."

She wanted to shout at him. She wanted more than that—what she'd really like, she thought then, was to take one of his priceless sculptures and throw it at his head.

But that would be another act of war.

And she was so tired of fighting.

So instead, she rose. Jolie found her feet and felt steadier when his gaze changed into something more like…arrested. As if he was no more sure of his power here than she was, no matter what he might claim. She crossed the space between them, moving over to his chair so she could sink down on her knees before him.

And she was glad that she had spent some time in this position, because if she hadn't, she might not have realized that it was not a surrender. She was not laying herself out before him in submission. Not when both of them knew how she could take her power here, rendering him little more than clay in her hands.

Not to mention what she could do with her mouth.

Part of the power, she understood now, was in the act of the surrender itself—not to him, but to what she believed was more important, here in this moment.

Not just Mathilde. She would always want to save her cousin, and she *would* make certain she did, but this wasn't only about her.

It was about *maybe*. It was about *what if.*

It was about the versions of them she glimpsed when they were too busy taking care of their guests to snipe at each other.

It was about the stories she wanted them to tell, years later, about these moments.

She knelt there before him and she reached over to take his hand between hers. It was the hand that wore a wider version of the simple band that she wore on hers. The evidence that they really were married. That it really had happened. That this wasn't all some fever dream of sex and laughter, golden nights and desperate, needy dawns.

There was so much tension in him. And all of that wild and unconquerable heat.

Jolie looked up at him, holding his gaze as surely as she held his hand. "I'm telling you everything because I want things to be different. I don't want there to be secrets between us. I want to try, you and me, to make something real out of this, Apostolis."

He stared at her, looking almost...frozen. But that was better than openly mocking. Or scathing.

So she pushed on. "What if we could start over? Without your father. Without battles and wars, weapons and forced marches and trenches neither one of us wants to be in. What if we could just...be ourselves? Not the people your father made, but whoever we want to be, you and me?"

His laugh was a thread of bitterness. "What an imagination you have."

"I have always known how you care for your sister," she said, with a sour hint of desperation in her mouth. "And even if I hadn't known it, even before we met, I now know that what you do is care for people. You've made it a business. You save people from disaster, Apostolis. And you came back home to save this hotel, too." She thought of all those photographs, lined up just so. "You care so much about these things that matter to you—your childhood home, your sister, the kind of good you do in the world. What if—" and she hated herself for the way her voice shook, or maybe she only wished she could hate the vulnerability that poured through her "—what if you let yourself care about us, too?"

And for a moment, all of those words seemed to dance there between them like their own kind of golden light, even though it was dark outside. It took Jolie a long moment to realize that it was one of the lights she'd switched on herself, flooding the pair of them where they sat.

That was when he leaned forward, flipping his hand so that he was the one holding her fast.

"The only time you tell the truth, my darling wife and favorite stepmother," and his voice was hoarse and so dark it made her shiver, "is when you come."

Something in her jolted in shock, as if her very bones were breaking.

Or maybe that was simply her heart.

"Apostolis. Please—"

"There are worse things than death, Jolie," he told her in that same dark voice. "Remember? Like losing. I hope you enjoy it."

And when his mouth came crashing down on hers, Jolie knew everything was lost.

But her deep tragedy was that she kissed him back.

CHAPTER TEN

APOSTOLIS FLEW TO Paris the next day, though he couldn't escape the feeling that he had not so much settled the issue between him and Jolie as postponed it.

They had exploded into their usual passion, but maybe that had been a mistake. It had all been...too much. Too real.

Or maybe it was his own weakness that so disgusted him.

Because he *wanted* to believe her. He wanted to believe it when she said those things about who they could be, about the kind of marriage they could have—

But he had given up on bedtime stories like that long ago.

And he had known the truth about Jolie from the first. He would be a weak man indeed if a pretty face changed his mind. He would be no better than his father.

He landed in Paris in a foul mood that the rain did not improve.

He met Alceu in one of the properties he kept in Paris, a town house a short walk from the Musée d'Orsay, and found his friend a curious reflection of his own odd frame of mind.

"You seem agitated," he told Alceu after they concluded the business that they'd ostensibly met to discuss.

"I am never agitated," his friend replied at once, making it clear enough to Apostolis that he was not quite himself. "You are the one who has the steam coming out of his ear. Is that not the phrase?"

As if Alceu did not know the damned phrase, fluent as he was in every language he encountered. But he did like to pretend otherwise for his own entertainment, and who was Apostolis to stand between his friend and his fun?

"What I cannot abide," Apostolis said instead, "is a liar who cannot determine that the time has come to stop spinning her stories."

But he regretted saying it instantly, because something in him...balked.

Rationally, it didn't make any sense. This was his oldest friend in the world. When he'd had no one, when his father had disowned him and made it clear that he was not permitted to come home, Alceu had been like a brother to him. Like more than a brother. They had forged their way through the world together. They had always, always stood tall at one another's backs.

He had always considered Alceu closer to him than his actual family.

All the same, something in him considered it the deepest kind of betrayal that he'd said even something so opaque about Jolie.

He understood in that moment that if she unburdened herself in a similar way to a friend of hers—or worse, his sister—even if she kept what she said as devoid of details, he would feel it like a knife in the gut.

And he could not say that he cared much for the way that realization made him feel, now that it was too late. Now that he'd said the thing he shouldn't have said. Maybe he'd needed to say such a thing to understand that things really had changed between him and Jolie, despite his protestations.

But she is *a liar,* a voice in him insisted.

Because the alternative was untenable.

Perhaps it was lucky that his friend seemed entirely preoccupied with the view of Paris outside his windows. A view that Alceu had seen before. Too many times to count.

"You seem unduly interested in the city tonight," Apostolis pointed out. "You must have developed a love for Paris that I did not think you possessed."

His friend did not turn back to face him. "I live at the top of a mountain. My nearest neighbors are trees. Sometimes it amazes me that so many people live like this. And on purpose."

Somehow, Apostolis didn't think that was it, though he knew better than to push. Alceu was less flexible than the mountain he lived on. "My sister said something similar." He laughed, remembering his last call with Dioni, who had managed to sound even more flighty and *Dioni* on what had sounded like the busiest street in Manhattan than before. "Did I not tell you that she has taken himself off to New York City, of all places, for the duration."

"I beg your pardon?"

Apostolis thought that Alceu seemed...even stiffer and more forbidding than usual, then. "I too was amazed that the little mouse would take herself off to the big city. I thought perhaps, one day, she might spend some time in Athens, I suppose, as many do. But New York?" He shrugged. "Yet as she tells it, it is as if she has never known home until now."

Alceu let out a laugh, then, and the sound made Apostolis frown. It was too bitter. It was...

But he never finished that thought, because Alceu turned around and was looking directly at him again, and his eyes were dark. And his voice was terse when he spoke. "As far as liars go, at a certain point it is better to choose to believe a lie if it leads to peace."

Apostolis blinked at that most unexpected statement from a man he would never have described as *peaceful* but Alceu was already moving, heading for the door as if responding to an alarm only he could hear.

"I beg your pardon, but I must go," Alceu bit off in that frozen way of his. "I forgot that there are some calls I must make."

And he shut the door behind him when he went in a manner that Apostolis thought boded ill for whoever it was he needed to call.

But he did not brood any further over his friend's behavior—or the odd thing he'd said about *peace*—once he'd gone. He moved over to the window himself and looked out at the scene that had so captivated Alceu. Paris at night, gleaming in the rain.

Yet he didn't see it. All he could think about was Jolie.

Jolie kneeling before him, whispering, *what if.*

And Jolie after that moment, spread out before him like one more decadent feast, giving all of herself to him. And murmuring things she should not while he took her, as if all of this was a different kind of story than the one he'd been telling himself all along—

But he could not accept it.

He would not.

The next day, he made a few calls. And as Alceu was nowhere to be found, he took leave of Paris and set off for Switzerland instead.

The last payment sent from Jolie's bank account had been to an address in Geneva, only two days before. It was time, he concluded, to find out the *real* truth. Then, perhaps, he would treat his darling wife to a few *what ifs* of his own design.

It was a short flight, and the closer he got, the more he felt that deep, dark, boiling fury inside of him.

He was certain that whatever he was about to find he would not like.

If she had not been a virgin, he would have assumed that she was supporting a lover. He could hear her as if she was sitting beside him on his plane, making arch comments about the power of her *built-in lie detector*.

Something about that seemed to shift inside him uneasily.

But he could not believe the things she had said to him. He could not believe she was simply an innocent, caught up in Spyros's game.

And then, the way she told it, in his.

He could not believe those things because if he did, he realized as his plan set down in Geneva, he would have to accept that he had not distanced himself from the old man the way he'd been so certain he had.

It should have been impossible that anyone could compare him to his father.

That it was not—

That thought was so horrifying that he found himself clenching his own jaw so tight that it was a wonder he didn't crack a tooth or two.

He had a car waiting for him and he stalked off the plane and into the backseat, letting the driver worry about getting him where he needed to go. Though that allowed him perhaps too much time to sit and consider the problem that was Jolie.

Apostolis didn't want to think about her. He didn't want to think about the seven years she had carried the hotel on her own slender shoulders. He did not want to think about the reading of his father's will. Or that stormy wedding that they had both surrendered to with such ill grace that their only two guests had removed themselves to get away from the vitriol between them.

He did not want to think of the years that stretched ahead of them still when it already seemed as if a lifetime had passed since his father had died and his vindictive intentions had been made clear.

There was only Jolie, for five whole years, if he wanted to claim his own birthright.

Then he thought about that birthright, too. And wondered why it hadn't occurred to him that it was an act of aggression on his father's part to have left nothing at all to Dioni.

Then again, argued a voice inside of him that

sounded suspiciously sharp, like Jolie's, *it's likely not* you *that he expected would take care of her. It's her friend. Her stepmother. Your wife. Spyros trusted her more than you, so does your own sister.*

In the back of the car, sliding along through the streets of Geneva, the lake gleaming at him and far-off mountain ranges standing proud. But he didn't see any of that. Apostolis felt his own chest vibrating and realized that he was actually *growling*.

Out loud.

He stopped at once.

Jolie wanted him to trust her. His own father had never trusted him, but then Apostolis had known better than to trust him. And he could not remember how or when that had started. It seemed to him that it had always been that way, since long before he had gained enough perspective on the world to make such a decision.

It felt like a simple gut feeling, and one he'd had his whole life.

Spyros was untrustworthy. Everything he did had deep, sharp talons attached and he never seemed to care who got cut. It was easy, even as a child, to make sure to keep away from that type of person.

He looked down at his hands, stretching them out as if looking for the blades attached to his own fingers that he was sure, suddenly, he could feel.

And then, perhaps inevitably, he thought of his mother.

Apostolis so rarely allowed himself that kind of nostalgia. When he thought of her, it was always from back when he was very small. When she had been a voice, soft and loving and instantly able to soothe him. He could remember the way she smelled like summer and that sometimes, when he passed the flowers that Jolie took such pride in arranging about the hotel, there were certain varieties that stopped him in his tracks.

Though he would never have admitted it.

Apostolis had never blamed his sister for his mother's death, though he wondered, now, if his father had. Because it would be just like Spyros to nurse a grudge for nearly thirty years, act as if he felt nothing but tender feelings for Dioni, and then wait for his will to do the real talking for him.

This, he assured himself, was why he insisted on uncovering Jolie's lies.

They both needed to know where they truly stood, always. So that there could be no pretending.

So that what happened to him once already could not occur again. He would not be, again, the recipient of a terse voice message from Spyros shortly before he'd finished university, letting him know that he was on his own. And was not welcome to return home until he could afford to get there himself.

I cannot imagine that this will surprise you, Spyros had said slyly. *You know how irresponsible you are, do you not?*

But he had known that it was a surprise. He had planned it that way.

If he was on his own, Apostolis preferred to know it from the start. There was a reason that the only per-

son he had ever trusted on this earth was Alceu, because they had proven themselves to each other. Time
and time again.

What was that saying? *Trust, but verify.*

That was all this was, he assured himself, as the car
pulled up in front of a block of flats in a neighborhood
nowhere near the beautiful views that Geneva was famous for. He frowned down at the address in his hand,
but told the driver to wait as he climbed out.

Then he strode to the door of the building, and wondered how, precisely, he planned to go about this—

But he didn't have to figure that out, because the
door opened as he stood there. A couple came out,
bickering in low, bitter tones.

He caught the door and brushed past them without
a second glance. Then, inside, he followed the stairs
up three flights until he found the flat number that he
had written down.

There was that band tied around his chest once more,
and much tighter than before. There was something
drumming in him, and he didn't like it.

Did he really want to knock on this door and have
his questions answered?

For a moment he wavered, thinking of those golden
nights out on the terrace, awash in starlight and wine.
The flush of music and something that felt like magic.

You know what that magic is, a voice in him whispered. *It's only that you don't want to admit it.*

He thought of Jolie climbing over him in the bed
they shared, moving over him like more of that same

perfect light, as if every time she touched him was an act of hope.

But here, in a downtrodden building in a questionable neighborhood in a city he had never particularly cared for, he shook that off.

This wasn't about hope. It was about truth.

He stomped forward and pounded on the door in question. He waited. And heard faint sound from inside, so he pounded again. Harder this time.

And he was ready when he heard the latch. He was ready when the door swung open. He would handle this, whatever it was, and if she thought that this would end their war, she would find he had been keeping the tanks and missiles at bay—

But then the door opened, just a sliver, and he stopped.

Everything in him *stopped*.

Because a girl stood there, looking back at him through the latched opening. He estimated that she was in her late teens or early twenties, and he recognized her immediately.

It was the eyes, far too blue for any land this far north. It was the hair, chopped short around her face, but still, a shade of sunshine he knew too well.

"If you're here for debt collection," the girl said, in a voice that sounded controlled enough, though he could see a bit of anxiousness in her expression, "I'm afraid that my parents have just left—"

Apostolis felt an earthquake rip through him, mercilessly. A fundamental, seismic shift. He had to reach 'out to steady himself on the doorjamb, and the girl's eyes widened.

"Don't be afraid," he managed to get out. "I won't hurt you. I am not here for *debt*."

And he had no idea how he would go about paying his. How he would ever manage to make up for the things he'd said.

The things he'd done, so convinced that Jolie was a villain.

"It's only that you look ill," the girl whispered. "You've gone pale. Are you going to be sick?"

"That," he gritted out, though he was surprised he could even speak through the upheaval inside of him, "would be an upgrade."

And he had to wait until the racket inside of him stilled. Not entirely. Just enough that he could feel the destruction and function anyway.

"I think I passed your parents on the way in," he said when he could speak without thinking it might knock him over. "Do you expect them back soon?"

She swallowed, but didn't answer—and he understood immediately.

"I'm sorry," he said at once. "I'm doing this all wrong. I am Apostolis Adrianakis. I am your cousin's husband, Mathilde. Jolie is my wife." And that he had claimed her like that, with no mocking aside, made everything in him shake anew. But he kept his eyes on Mathilde. The girl Jolie had given so much of herself for. How could he do any less? "It is time for you to be free."

Then he held out his hand and waited for Jolie's cousin to take it.

As if, once she did, it might redeem him.

CHAPTER ELEVEN

JOLIE WAS MAKING her way back up from one of the villages, her arms full of flowers, when she saw Apostolis's plane fly in overhead.

She told herself—sternly—that there was absolutely no call for the leap of hope in her chest. He had made himself abundantly clear when he'd left. He hadn't even told her where he'd gone.

It was the height of foolishness to think that whatever he'd done when he was away—for two interminable nights, during which she'd slept a combined five minutes, so impossible was it to sleep without him—might have changed his thinking in any way.

But she didn't feel the least bit tired now. And she couldn't deny that there was a spring in her step as she made her way back up the winding steps, cut into the hillside, that the locals took from the nearest village to the Andromeda.

She ordered herself to slow down. To take care with the flowers she was carrying to make an extra arrangement that she'd decided to put in the bedroom of one of their guests, a young girl who reminded her of Mathilde.

And herself, she supposed.

Both of them, maybe, if none of the things that had happened to them had been permitted to occur.

Maybe she wanted to celebrate that in another wide-eyed girl before her own life gave her reasons to stop smiling.

She got back to the hotel where there were questions to answer, small fires to extinguish, and then the flowers to arrange in the kitchen and send up to the girl's room.

Jolie wished that she could have lost herself in all of those things, instead of listening for that Range Rover on the drive. Or looking around every time a door opened, thinking it would be him.

She supposed that this was only to be expected. Some kind of Stockholm syndrome—or maybe it was the sex that was addictive. Never in her life had she felt more like a junkie than the last two nights without.

Or maybe she was simply *used to him* by now. She'd had time to think about that, these last couple of nights, lying all alone in that bed that seemed entirely too large and empty without him.

She couldn't sleep when he was gone, and that had shocked her. She kept waking up, reaching for him, and he wasn't there.

And there were two ways that she could think about that. One, that she was deeply pathetic to allow herself to have these kinds of feelings for someone who was more often cruel to her than not.

But the other way of looking at it was that they had been fighting their way toward each other all this time. And maybe, just maybe, she just needed to fight a little longer.

For how could she know how delusional she was until he returned?

When she was finished with her tasks, she let herself out the side door of the hotel and started for the carriage house, her pulse skyrocketing because she saw the Range Rover parked there in front.

He was home. He really was *here.*

And now she would have to decide which part of her poor heart was right, after all.

Jolie couldn't seem to stop her feet from moving and that was terrible, because right then, she thought she would give anything to stop time. To keep *not knowing,* because what if he gave her an answer that she couldn't live with?

What would she do then?

She hardly recognized herself as she raced across the drive, heedless for once of how it might look to anyone who might be watching. She was practically transfigured with desperation and something too sharp to truly be hope as she wrenched open the door and all but fell into the hall.

Into all those black-and-white photographs, all those frozen moments. All those possibilities of joy and life and light that she'd always felt was out of her reach.

As if she was stuck on the other side of a glass frame forever, always looking in, never a part of it.

That was not the story she wanted any longer. Not from Apostolis.

Not now that she'd started listening to her heart again, for the first time in a decade.

Jolie walked deeper into the house, already fairly certain that she knew the answer, because he wasn't there to greet her. He wasn't there at all, and her stomach twisted. Everything inside her urged her to turn and run. To hide somewhere, so she could still pretend that this might go the way she wanted it to go.

But she didn't.

And she was halfway across the grand, flowing space when she heard a noise and looked up—

To see him coming down the winding stair.

"Apostolis," she began, because she couldn't seem to keep his name inside of her, and there were so many other things that she wanted to say before he started in—

"We will talk, you and I," he told her in a low voice. "But there is something that I think you must do first."

"I don't want to do anything else, I just want to say—"

But he didn't come toward her. He stopped at the bottom of the stair and he didn't even cut her off with an impatient slash of his hand, or even his mouth on hers. All he did was lift a finger and point toward the gallery.

Jolie felt frozen solid, but she followed the line his finger suggested, looking up.

And then she stopped breathing, because there against the wall of art and sculpture stood a slim blonde figure.

"Mathilde," she whispered.

"Is it true?" her cousin asked her, her voice barely above a whisper, though it seemed to reverberate within Jolie like a shout. "Is it really true that I can simply come to you now, and live with you, and be free of them forever? He says that I can do this. That he has made it happen." Mathilde's face crumpled. "Oh, Jolie, tell me it's true."

And all Jolie could do was throw a shocked and overjoyed look Apostolis's way—because she was already moving, racing up those stairs, winding herself around and around until she burst out at the gallery level and took her cousin in her arms.

In a hug that she hoped would go on forever.

They made a good start.

And it was a long while later that she left Mathilde in the guest room that she had once tried to claim as her own, surrounded by the things that Apostolis had brought here with her.

Mathilde had told her an impossible story of Apostolis appearing at her door and ordering her to pack her things, which she had done with alacrity, because she'd recognized him. She'd seen the photographs and the commentary in the papers.

None of which I believed, of course, she assured Jolie, who did not know how to tell her younger cousin that she had not given a single thought to the gossips in ages. *They only make money on scandalous innuendo. I know you better than that.*

You do, she had agreed, beckoning her to continue.

She did. Even more improbably, Apostolis had stood between Mathilde and her parents when they'd returned and had made it abundantly clear to them that they were not only cut off from Jolie's money, but that it would be in their best interest to disappear entirely. Because, according to Apostolis, fleets of attorneys were already preparing to make sure that the rest of their lives were even more of a misery than they could expect if left to their own devices.

And more, that Jolie was off-limits. Mathilde's eyes had been so wide that they almost took over her face as she related each and every word that had been spoken.

And then he told them that I was off-limits, too, she had said. With reverence. *He said, 'If I were you, I would go away and stay gone.'*

Neither Mathilde nor Jolie could imagine that they would follow this advice, but one thing was certain— that particular reign of terror was over. At least for them.

Because Mathilde's parents would have to go through Apostolis now.

And that changed everything.

A long while later, Jolie left her cousin to settle in— and, she hoped, sleep off all the excitement and the travel and dream about the possibility that this long nightmare was truly over now. She went out into the hall, her pulse kicking into high gear.

It was time to find him.

It's finally time, she thought as she let herself into the master bedroom, but he wasn't there. She had to stop and breathe a little before she started hyperventilating.

Or sobbing.

When she thought she could keep herself together, she picked her way downstairs again, expecting that she would find him in the office. But he wasn't there either.

There was a kind of panic growing within her as she made her way outside and across the drive to the hotel. But when she checked into the kitchens and offices where the staff congregated, there were the usual tasks and issues to handle, but no one mentioned Apostolis—which meant that he wasn't already there, handling things.

Had he left again? Jolie couldn't believe that.

When she went outside again, she stopped in the yard. The ocean breeze picked up the length of her hair and played with it. There were guests down by the pool, so she smiled and waved.

But she didn't see Apostolis there with them, so she went the other way. She walked up to the edge of the cliff, where there were benches placed for taking in the sea. And that was where she saw him at last.

He was down below, standing alone in the rocky cove down at sea level where that picture of him and Dioni had been taken a lifetime ago.

Jolie started toward the stairs that had been carved into the side of the cliff to lead the family and now the guests down to the water, but by the time she reached them she was running. She hurtled her way down them as if every moment apart from him was torture—

Because it is, she thought, feeling almost feverish.

And then she was on the beach herself, running toward him.

It was reckless. She knew that.

But the truth was that she didn't care how they'd left things. She wasn't sure it would have mattered *before* she'd seen who he'd come home with. Now it couldn't.

All that mattered was that he'd brought her Mathilde.

Jolie didn't care why or how he'd done it, only that he had.

So when he turned, looking back over his shoulder just before she reached him, she didn't think.

She launched herself toward him with every confidence that he would catch her.

With *faith*.

With trust, because sometimes thinking about things made it more complicated than it was.

Jumping in the air wasn't complicated. It was a yes or no question.

And he answered it.

He caught her. And he held her tight in his arms for a moment, there against his chest.

And he looked as if it hurt him when he set her back down on the ground.

"*Apostolis.*" She breathed his name like a prayer. A prayer he had also answered. "How can I thank you enough? Thank you. *Thank you.* Thank—"

"Stop," he urged her, though it was in a different sort of voice than the one he'd used that last night, so bitter and dark, when she'd knelt before him and believed that all was lost.

Herself most of all.

"Apostolis," she tried again. "Please, you must—"

"I flew across Europe to prove you're a liar," he told

her in that low, bittersweet voice. His gaze was so dark it made a lump grow in her throat. "Yet all I found was the truth, exactly as you'd told it to me. And the whole way back, while your cousin backed up all you told me and shared a good deal you did not, all I could think of was what you've been through. What you had gone to such trouble to save her from." He shook his head. "What my father must have done to you, all of these years. I have no doubt that he was imaginative. And vile. He always is."

She held on to him as if the sea might sneak in if she wasn't careful and steal him away.

"Your father is dead," she told him, her gaze on his. "There's no need to keep digging up his grave."

He made as if to put space between them at that, but she held on. And she could see that familiar light of battle in his gaze, but for the first time, it occurred to her that his first fight, always, was with himself.

As hers was with herself, too.

Because neither one of them had wanted this, and yet here they were, drawn together yet again.

"I don't want to dig up any graves, but I don't know how to begin to apologize to you," Apostolis told her, his voice almost too low to hear over the surf. But then, she thought she would be able to hear him anywhere. He was already etched into her skin. Her bones. Maybe it had always been a kind of arrogant foolishness to pretend otherwise. "I don't even know where to start. I can think of nothing else—but it has finally occurred to me what has to be done."

She frowned at him, still gripping the inside of his

arms. "You can't divorce me. You can't even leave me effectively. It's right there, in the will."

His mouth curved, just slightly. And her treacherous heart, which should have been left in tiny little pieces too small to ever come together again, blossomed into a brand-new kind of hope.

"I owe you a reckoning," he said quietly. "Because I am the liar here, not you."

She found herself whispering his name.

"Seven years ago I did not give you marital advice, such as it was, out of the goodness of my heart," he told her as if he was making a confession before a court. "I took one look at you and told myself that I disliked you on sight. But I didn't."

"I was there, Apostolis. You did."

He shook his head, and there was gold in his gaze again. "My darling wife. My favorite stepmother." He ran a hand over her hair as if he marveled at the feel of it, just as she gloried in his touch. "I felt something at first sight, but it was not *dislike*. And it was not allowed. I believe that in that moment I decided that you must be evil if I could fall like that, and therefore a liar by definition. I excused myself, of course."

She thought of running down the steps to the beach. Of tossing herself so heedlessly into his arms. There were a thousand things she could have said, but all of them were ways to fight—because she thought she had to fight to protect the soft parts of her she kept inside.

But she'd already told him what she wished for. What did she have to keep safe now that she'd already exposed herself?

"I excuse you now," she said softly.

"You shouldn't," he returned, sounding almost out-raged at the idea. "There are so many more lies. I told myself I hated you when, in fact, you are the only woman I have ever wanted enough to make me weak. To make me behave like this. This monster who has more in common with his father than I ever imagined possible. If I am honest, Jolie, I am disgusted with myself."

"This is why we have to stop these wars," she said, her eyes stinging with the effort of keeping her tears at bay. "Because all they do is tear us apart. Just imagine—"

"I have imagined very little else," he told her, hoarsely. "But I will tell you now, I don't deserve it. I will never deserve it. When I think of the things that you deserve, none of them involve me. The son of the man who treated you this way. The man who, all on his own, in some ways treated you worse."

But Jolie shook her head, moving even closer to him.

"Arguing with you has always been like a dance. I don't want to lose the spark of it." She shook her head, not sure she believed that she'd said that out loud...but then she realized that it was true. There were years that she had lived for his few visits and the opportunity to fence a few words and fake smiles with this man. After the will was read, after their wedding, she would be lying if she claimed there wasn't a part of her that was thrilled they got to poke at each other the way they did. And she could have moved herself right back to the back house. She hadn't. Because she'd wanted the ex-citement of waiting to see what he'd say next. Or what she'd say back. "All I want is for it to be different. To be about us, not about him. Do you think that's possible?"

He was shaking his head, as if she was causing him pain. "What I don't know is why you would want it to be possible. Why you would want any of this at all."

"Because," Jolie said quietly, as if it was a secret between her and him and the sea, "whenever I think of love, I think of you. Not because we found that, you and me. But because I want it from you. Because I want the *what ifs,* and the *maybes,* and all those nights we pretended to be real. I want to see where that goes. I want all those possibilities, Apostolis. I know you think that's losing the war, but I think—"

He whispered her name, like some kind of incantation.

"Nothing is worse than losing you," he told her. "Not even death. I would lose a thousand wars, every day, as long as I had this. As long as I have you."

He leaned in and kissed her. And it was sweet and light—until she kissed him deeper. More urgently.

Because sweet and light was not who they were.

She wanted him. All of him.

"I'm so sorry," he said against her mouth, between tasting her and teasing her, and making her feel like she was home at last. "I don't know the first thing about loving anyone, but I promise you, whatever I have in me, it's yours."

"I know even less," she told him, wrapping herself around him. "So we will have to do it together, you and me."

"My darling wife," he said, "my only stepmother, *asteri mou*, I am yours."

"And I am only and ever yours," she replied.

The next time they kissed, right there on that beach, was the beginning.

The end of the war.

And the beginning of *forever*.

CHAPTER TWELVE

THEY PRIDED THEMSELVES on falling a little more in love every day.

They worked on it.

They did not keep score—though Apostolis took some time before he forgave himself.

Jolie was quicker.

But then, she had a secret weapon.

When things did not seem to be going in the right direction, all she needed to do was smile in that sharp, barbed way that never failed to get his attention.

"Are you certain you wish to smile at me like that?" he would ask, dangerously.

"You sound like a small man making big noises," she said once in response—

And then laughed and laughed when he swept her up and tossed her, fully dressed, into the pool.

Then spent a good deal longer kissing her dry in the privacy of their bedroom.

Because they liked a spark. They would never run out of their fire.

She wouldn't know them if they did.

Mathilde settled into life at the Andromeda beautifully. At first she didn't want to leave Jolie's side. The two of them spent hours and hours together, first comparing notes. Then building new memories.

And it was no more than a couple of years later that Mathilde came to them and said that she thought it was time she tried a bit of independence—and she knew just the place.

Because by then they all knew about Dioni's adventures in New York.

"I cannot quite get my head around choosing a concrete city when there is all this," Apostolis confessed one evening.

The sunset was settling in, spectacularly. The guests had drifted out from the terrace to gather at the cliffside, the better to truly take it in.

"Everyone must find their own path, my love," Jolie told him.

He looked down at her, that smile on his face that was only hers. "As long as your path always leads to me, *latria mou*."

Jolie let him pull her into his side as the sun put on its nightly show. Later, there would be dancing. It was that kind of night. Later still, they would walk back across the drive and laugh as they found each other in the dark hall.

They had no secrets left. He knew she understood Greek. She knew every last detail of his dealings with Alceu and the soft heart he kept hidden so deep inside of him.

There was only one thing that she was hiding from him, but it was new.

And she resolved she would tell him. Tonight.

Later, when they were both naked and breathing too hard, she turned so she could prop herself up on his chest and look deep into his fathomless eyes. And so both of them could bathe in all the moonlight pouring in the windows.

"I have something to tell you," she said. Solemnly.

Apostolis smiled. "I was wondering when you would get around to it."

She felt her smile bubble up from the deepest place inside of her. "Of course you know."

"My darling wife," he said, kissing her in between each word, "my favorite stepmother, *fos tis psihis mou,* I love you. I know everything about you. It is my religion."

And then, together, they shifted so they could both smooth their hands over her only very slightly rounded belly.

"This baby will be born a month after our five years is up," she told him, old ghosts dancing around them but not getting close.

There was too much fire between them for that.

"Good," he said, pulling her mouth back to his. "Now you will be stuck with me forever."

But he was laughing while he said it, and she was laughing, too, because they knew the only truth that mattered.

Forever, for them, was only the beginning. This baby would only be their first.

And their legacy would be love and it would stand

the test of time, until long after the Andromeda was nothing but rubble.

That was the story Jolie liked best.

So together, day after day, they made it come true.

* * * * *

Did Greek's Enemy Bride *leave you wanting more? Then you're bound to love the next instalment in the Notorious Mediterranean Marriages duet, coming soon!*

And while you wait, why not dive into these other Caitlin Crews stories?

A Tycoon Too Wild to Wed
Her Venetian Secret
Pregnant Princess Bride
Forbidden Royal Vows
Greek's Christmas Heir

Available now!

   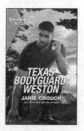